DARK EMPORIUM – VOLUME 1

Edited by Misty Coleman

DARK EMPORIUM – VOLUME 1

GRAVESTONE PRESS

TABLE OF CONTENTS

Sapphire Eyes Shining (Rie Sheridan Rose)

Cody slammed the flat of his hand down on the edge of his desk, sending a stack of textbooks spinning to the floor with a hollow clatter. "You can't do this to me! I worked hard on that paper."

"Mr. Eilers, we both know the hardest work you did on the paper was photocopying your research and rearranging the order of the information." Professor Warner rose from his perch on the corner of his own paper-strewn desk and moved behind it.

Cody's eyes narrowed. The "power position." Yeah, well, he'd read the psych books too. He moved forward to lean over the professor's desk. "This is unfair, and you know it."

"What I 'know' is you can do better work than this. I also realize your grant rides on this class, so I am going to give you a chance to redo the paper. You have until 8 o'clock sharp on Monday morning to turn it in to me."

"But it's Friday afternoon. That doesn't give me enough time!"

"You had three weeks to prepare the paper the first time. If you wasted your research opportunity and plagiarized your results instead, you can hardly construe that as my fault. If you prefer, I can take the matter to the Dean at once."

Cody scowled, sweeping his blond hair out of his eyes with an angry swipe of his hand. "I'll do it." He thrust out his hand for the paper Professor Warner held.

"No, Mr. Eilers. I'll just hang on to this draft."

"But all my references—"

"Surely you have another copy of your bibliography. If not, I suggest you get started." Professor Warner glanced down at his wristwatch. "It's almost 6:00. The library closes at 10:00 on Friday. That is all. Dismissed."

Cody shoved back his chair. It grated across the tile floor with a harsh screech as he bent to collect his books, slamming them into his knapsack with haphazard abandon. He threw a sullen glare in Professor Warner's direction, but the instructor graded papers as if the young man did not exist. Cody got the message, storming out of the office, and slamming the door hard enough to rattle the frosted glass.

"How did it go?" Mary Ann asked, her voice anxious as she rose from the hallway bench where she had been waiting.

"He's making me redo the whole goddamn paper."

"And…?"

"Isn't that enough?" He whirled on her, furious she didn't seem to understand. "It'll take me all weekend! I don't have time to waste on this crap."

"I'll help you, Cody," she soothed, laying a tentative hand on his tensed arm. "Come on…if we go to the library now, I bet we could get enough sources by closing—"

8

"I'll do it tomorrow. I've got things to do tonight."

"But Cody—"

"Look, you can come with me or not," he growled, giving her an emerald stare that would freeze lava, "but I'm not wasting *my* Friday night in the goddamn library."

Mary Ann ducked her head, her dark hair obscuring her face. "Sure, Cody," she whispered. "Whatever you say."

The ice in his eyes melted, and he slipped a finger under her chin, tilting her head up. "I'm sorry, sweetheart," he murmured. "I know it's not your fault. You tried to warn me." He released a gusty sigh. "I guess I just didn't believe the prick would catch on." He threw an arm across her slim shoulders. "C'mon. Let's go downtown." He slung the knapsack over his back and led her out of the building.

April wound down toward May, making for a beautiful day. The days lengthened with the approach of summer, and the golden light lay across the campus in a warm blanket.

Mary Ann darted a quick look up at Cody, a half-smile fluttering around her lips. He whistled a Warren Zevon song as they walked, winking down at her. The smile blossomed fully, transforming her thin face.

Cody returned the smile, but his thoughts remained on Professor Warner. He had screwed up this time. He only had a light nine-hour semester to go, and he'd finally get certified, but he couldn't afford to stay at the Center without his grant.

9

This close to the end, he'd been a *maniac* to rip off a paper! Especially for Warner's class. Everyone knew the Professor was a stickler for originality. But there'd been a project due in his Film Editing class that day as well, and he'd spent every waking moment for the entire three weeks working on it instead.

He and Mary Ann walked the short distance from the campus to his apartment, and Cody threw his knapsack into the rear seat of his beat-up Mustang instead of going inside the building. The car had a classic body, but it had to be cajoled and babied to start. "Shall we give Amanda here a try, or take the train?"

"Whatever you want, Cody," she said with a shrug.

He felt a flash of irritation. Sometimes Mary Ann was so damn pliable he wanted to shake her...but he could always rely on her. He grinned at her across the ragtop of the car. "I guess we should take the train then, kiddo. There's plenty of daylight left. Let's go exploring. Try someplace we haven't been before." He loved to wander the streets of downtown, particularly the art galleries and the funky little hole-in-the-wall outlets. It had a way of calming the storm that sometimes blew through him....

Cody and Mary Ann strolled arm and arm to the nearest BMT station, and he flipped two tokens into the box. Though crowded with early commuters, he found Mary Ann a seat in the car, holding onto the strap above her head.

"Cody...don't you think we should work on your paper—?" she ventured nervously.

"I told you before," he answered tightly, his knuckles whitening around the strap as he fought to control his temper. "I'm *not* wasting my Friday night on that jerk's assignment."

"So, you'll waste all day Saturday instead?" she mumbled, so softly he had to strain to hear her.

His blood instantly exploded, the anger pounding Morse code behind his eyes. "Look, Mary Ann—"

The argument continued to escalate—Mary Ann gently placating and Cody furiously volatile. Neither noticed the stops flashing by until they were miles beyond their intended destination.

"Great!" Cody growled, glancing up at last. "We're almost to the goddamn tunnel." He jerked her to her feet and jostled his way to the front of the car. When the doors opened at the next stop, he pushed her out of the car, keeping a firm grip on her arm so she wouldn't fall.

"Where are we, Cody?" she asked meekly, glancing around them curiously as they emerged back into the late afternoon sunlight.

"Canal somewhere," he shrugged. A grin split his face, brightening his sullen features into something almost magical. "Let's check it out. It's still early yet." He laced an arm around her waist. "How 'bout some Chinese?" he tempted, knowing the quickest way to her stomach was Oriental.

"Sure." The mood swings were as much a part of Cody as his name, and they had to be accepted if she wanted a continued relationship.

They walked east along Canal toward Chinatown, stopping often to glance into a shop window. By the time they hit Mountain, Cody had worked off the last of his irritation, leading the way south into the heart of Chinatown. They wandered through the maze of little streets leading off the principal thoroughfares. On Bai Jin Street, they found a dusty doorway, half hidden between two empty storefronts. The sign beside the open door said, "Welcome," and Cody felt drawn to the dim interior.

"Let's go in here."

Mary Ann pulled back. "Can't you smell that, Cody?" she wheedled, pointing to a restaurant two doors down. The scent of Oriental spices hung in the air, tantalizing the senses.

"In a minute, Mary Ann...I just want to look in here." He stepped across the threshold of the tiny store. The space stretched away down a center aisle to a glass counter at the far end. High banks of shelves lined both sides of the aisle, crowded with intriguing glimpses of half-recognized merchandise. Cody felt a shiver of delight run through him. It felt as if he'd been here before...and something here waited for him to take it away. He knew that with unshakable certainty.

Cody started down the narrow aisle, glancing at the items on the shelves, stopping now and then to touch something that caught his attention. "C'mon...look at this place. It's awesome!"

Mary Ann hung back by the door; her arms crossed protectively across her chest. "Cody, I really think we should get going—"

At that precise moment, he found it. As surely as if it had spoken his name. He reached down and picked up a small black jeweler's box, flipping open the lid to reveal a heavy silver ring in the shape of a coiled snake. The detail was incredible—each minuscule scale well-defined, and the delicate head smiling a serpent's grin. The eyes were two glittering green stones.

He had to have it.

Cody carried the small box over to the dusty glass counter, never taking his eyes off the snake. He noticed more and more detail—the faint suggestion of a folded hood, the infinitesimal tip of a fang peeking out from the curved mouth. He found it exquisite.

When he reached the counter, he glanced into the shadows behind it. No one appeared to be in the storefront, though a shimmering bead curtain over a rear doorway led into even murkier depths.

"Hello?" he called. "Is anybody there?"

"Cody…let's go—please," Mary Ann urged from the front of the store, edging toward the freedom of the open street.

"In a sec, okay? Hello?" Cody called again, his voice gaining confidence. "I'd like to buy something. Hello!"

A whisper of sound came from somewhere behind the curtain, and then it parted. A man stepped into the shop from the darkness beyond. Though definitely Asian, Cody couldn't determine his country of origin.

His hair appeared the black of a starless night, flowing sleekly into a neat queue. He wore a silk jacket of midnight blue worked with gold stars over ballooning black trousers, and Cody grinned to himself. What a tourist monger....

And then he saw the man's eyes.

Those eyes were ageless, depthless, and timeless. Two calm reflecting pools of jet set into a face unlined and yet ancient. Cody almost put down the box and fled...but he shook himself mentally and held it up instead.

"How much for this ring? There's no price on it."

The man cocked his head in a quizzical gesture and held out a hand for the box. "A beautiful piece. Ancient."

"Are those emeralds in its eyes?"

"No, corundum—a variety of the stone you call 'sapphire.'"

"I thought sapphires were blue," Cody challenged.

"Sapphire comes in many shades. They sometimes call this color 'oriental emerald.'" The man turned the box in his hand, staring down at it with a thoughtful expression. "Are you *sure* you wish to purchase this?"

"Uh, yeah," Cody mumbled, confused by having his doubts put into words. "How much?"

"First, make sure it fits, young sir. No use buying the ring if you cannot wear it, no?"

Cody flushed, the color staining his tan. "Oh, yeah...makes sense." Hand trembling with desire, he slipped the heavy silver circlet out of its box and eased it onto his left hand. The ring fit snugly, hugging his finger. The weight of it felt sensual—

14

right somehow—as if it was something he'd missed without ever being aware it was gone.

"It does seem made for you," the man murmured, his words a soft sigh tinged with a trace of inexplicable sadness. "That will be $20."

"No way!" Cody crowed, reaching for his wallet before the man could change his mind.

The ring had to be worth far more than that— why such a good deal…? He dragged a worn bill from the Velcro billfold, afraid the shopkeeper might wise up before the deal was final. "Here you go, mister."

"They call me the Caretaker." The shopkeeper gave a slight bow from the waist. "May you find wisdom in your purchase," the man proclaimed, brow creased with a cryptic frown. "We shall not meet again." He turned and walked back toward the rear of the shop.

"Oh, I don't know. You've got a lot of cool stuff in here. I may be back."

The Caretaker glanced back over his shoulder as he paused at the bead curtain, and Cody felt a sudden chill run through him. "No. I think not, young sir. May you find peace along the path you have chosen."

The man's oblique sayings grated on Cody's nerves. "Whatever," he growled impatiently, turning toward the doorway. "You can keep the box. I'll wear it out."

The Caretaker gave a single nod and disappeared behind his curtain once more.

Cody bounced down the aisle to the front of the shop. Mary Ann had stepped outside the doorway, and now huddled on the sidewalk outside the shop, hugging herself and shivering.

"Hey, babe, you cold?" Cody threw his left arm around her shoulders, and she surreptitiously moved to his other side. "What's wrong with you?" he growled, rolling his eyes impatiently.

"N-nothing. I just want to walk over here…I can watch the street…."

Cody shrugged. "Whatever." He wouldn't let her spoil his evening. "Come on. That Chinese smells better than ever. How 'bout some General Tso's?" he quipped. His accent was atrocious.

Mary Ann giggled, as he'd known she would— it was an old and comfortable joke. "Tso what?" she responded on cue, matching his pronunciation.

He leaned over and brushed a kiss on the top of her head. "Tso how about coming home with me later?" he purred seductively, and she threw her arms about his waist, hugging him hard.

His arm tightened about her shoulders. Many of his friends wondered about his choice of "plain Jane" Mary Ann, but he truly admired the fragile spirit hidden like a pearl inside her thin frame. She was all his, and the thought was a fiercely protective one. He'd make sure it always stayed that way.

After dinner and a return ride on a now nearly empty subway, Cody and Mary Ann cuddled on his overstuffed sofa. His hand played with her silky nightshade hair as they talked—until she let out a soft cry.

"Cody…that hurts!"

He looked down to see several long strands wound tight in the coils of the silver ring. "I'm sorry, sweetheart," he apologized, carefully extricating the ring. "Maybe I should take this thing off." He tugged gently at the band, then frowned.

It wouldn't come off.

He pulled harder, grunting at the unexpected twinge of pain that resulted. He finally gave up with a shrug. "Sorry, kiddo. I guess my finger's a little swollen. It won't come off right now. I'll just try to be more careful." He reached for her again, but Mary Ann slid gracefully from his arms and stood.

"That's okay, Cody.... It's late. I'd better get home."

"I thought you were going to stay—"

"I-I know, but I've got some studying to do...and tomorrow we've got to work on your paper..." Still making excuses, she gathered up her purse and denim jacket, starting for the door.

"Sure...if that's what you want," Cody muttered through tight lips, following her to the door. "Guess I'll see you in the morning, then."

"Yeah...I'll meet you at the library." She kissed him swiftly, then slipped out the door into the soft spring night.

"Well, I'm not wasting what's left of my Friday night sitting here alone," Cody commented to the empty room, grabbing his own jacket and keys. With a great deal of coaxing, he got the Mustang started and drove uptown to a favorite bar. A couple of beers would just about hit the spot, he decided, grinning in anticipation.

He locked the car and sauntered into O'Riley's. The bar was dark—heavy black walnut wainscoting and forest green wallpaper lit by smoky topaz

17

lamps. The bar counter itself was an imported antique of polished mahogany with a marble top and brass rails. Cody liked O'Riley's because it let him pretend he had left the city and traveled off to some crowded London pub.

He leaned against the chest-high bar and called out to the bartender. "Hey, Sam! Draw me up a malt?"

"Sure, Cody." The man set a frosted mug in front of him, and Cody took it to his favorite booth in the back corner. He slowly sipped the heavy draft, absently watching a dart game going on across the room.

"What are you looking at, punk?" growled one of the dart players belligerently. The man was taller and heavier than Cody, and obviously quite drunk.

"Just watching the game," replied Cody mildly, voice consciously pitched to be inoffensive. "I'm sorry—I didn't realize you'd mind."

"Well, I do mind." The man stepped closer, spoiling for a fight. "So, what are you going to do about it?"

"Stop watching the game, I guess." Cody shrugged, turning away deliberately to study the reproduction heraldry chart tacked to the wall beside the booth.

"Hey!" Cody felt a heavy hand descend on his shoulder and stiffened. "I'm not through with you, kid!"

"Please take your hand off my shoulder," Cody warned. His blood began the quick climb to its boiling point. If the man hadn't been drunk, he might have sensed Cody's mood and backed off.

Instead, he clipped Cody on the side of the head with the flat of his hand. "That better?" he chortled.

Cody sprang to his feet in one fluid motion and brought his fist around to connect with the man's jaw. The heavy silver ring impacted with a solid thud and the man staggered back, cradling his jaw with one hand. An odd look crossed his face, and he spat a tooth into his cupped palm.

"Why you little fuck—" he snarled thickly, advancing toward Cody, who dropped into an instinctive crouch, ready for the fight.

A loud crack sent both combatants springing back a pace. Sam stepped between them with an aluminum baseball bat. "Party's over, boys. Time to call it a night."

"Sam, I didn't—" Cody protested.

"Go home, Cody. It's for the best."

Cody started to protest further but decided not to risk making the banishment permanent. "All right." He scooped up his beer and drained it in a gulp, eyeing Sam defiantly, then stalked out of the bar.

Tonight turned out to be an A-1 disaster all around. He seethed, jamming his key into the door of the Mustang and flinging it open. Slamming the door closed behind him, he threw the car into gear. For once, Amanda behaved herself and started right up. Cody peeled out of the tiny parking lot and sped back to the apartment, half-daring a policeman to stop him.

When he got home, he paced the living room, too angry to settle down. Finally, he threw himself down on the couch; one arm flung over his eyes and forced himself to relax. Gradually, his iron will subjugated his anger, and he fell into a troubled sleep.

He dreamed of the bully from the bar; voice slurred with drink as he accosted Cody. In the dream, Cody simply smiled. Stepping aside, he revealed a huge, gleaming mamba with scales of polished silver coiled to strike. The man's eyes widened with fear, and he turned to run—jabbering incoherent prayers as he fled—but the snake moved like lightning and caught him before he'd gone a hundred yards. It reared back to strike, sinking needle-sharp fangs into the man's shoulder. The bully screamed in agony, and Cody's soul echoed the sound with a howl of triumph.

The dream proved so realistic Cody jerked up, heart pounding. It didn't seem right to feel so good about another's death, even if only in a dream…but it had been *so* satisfying—almost orgasmic. He scrubbed at his sweat-drenched face with his left hand, as if trying to wipe away the remnants of the experience.

It took him a moment to realize his hand was unexpectedly bare. He looked down at it dully, thoughts too sleep-muddled at first to realize the significance; then he bolted off the couch in alarm.

"Shit!" He searched among the sofa cushions, frantically running his fingers into the cracks. "Think!" he ordered himself, closing his eyes. "When did I have it last…?"

He remembered the ring connecting with the dart player's jaw and hoped it hadn't fallen off at the bar. "Have I seen it since then?" He concentrated hard, trying to recall.

When he had gotten home, he remembered there had been a tug as it caught on a loose thread inside the sleeve of his jacket. He sprang to the coat rack beside the door, grabbing the jacket and shaking it. "Damn!" he swore, throwing the garment to the floor when he failed to find the ring.

"Where could it be?" He slumped down on the edge of the sofa, head cradled in his hands, his brief burst of energy strangely exhausted. "Find it later…" he mumbled, the thought trailing off into sleep as he fell back onto the cushions.

Several hours later, Cody awakened to a tentative knock on the door. "W-what time is it?" he groaned, bringing his left arm around to look at his watch. He had to blink several times until the numbers swam into focus. Almost noon. Shaking his head, he sat up, groggy from either too much or too little sleep—he wasn't sure which.

Cody dropped his face into his hands and took a deep breath. He had to pull himself together…. Standing up to go to the door, he happened to glance down at his left hand. The ring was in its place on his finger.

"What the…? It must have been part of my dream…" he reasoned, relieved not to have lost it.

He opened the door, and Mary Ann stood on the threshold, hand poised to knock again. "Are you okay?" she asked anxiously.

"Sure. Why?"

"It's after 11:30. We were supposed to meet at the library at 9:00 to work on your paper."

"Oh, jeez! I forgot. I was asleep…."

"Rough night?"

"Kinda." He stepped away from the door. "Come in while I grab a shower. I promise I'll spend the rest of the day working on the paper." Cody raised one hand in the traditional Boy Scout salute.

Mary Ann laughed. "I've got a few sources for you, Scout," she commented as she moved past him into the room.

"You're a lifesaver, sweetheart. I won't take over five minutes, tops."

"Okay."

He hurried into the bedroom, grabbing a clean pair of jeans and a tee shirt.

"I brought in the newspaper," Mary Ann called. "I thought maybe we could take a break later for a movie."

"Sounds good to me. Look for something you want to see." He stepped into the shower, letting the cold spray revive him. "Much better," he mumbled to himself, quickly finishing his shower and getting dressed. He came out of the bedroom toweling his wet hair just as Mary Ann let out an exclamation.

"What is it, hon?" he asked curiously.

"Isn't O'Riley's the bar you like so much?"

"Yeah. Why?" A sudden sinking feeling roiled in the pit of his stomach.

"Says here someone dropped dead in their parking lot last night."

"Really?"

"Yeah. He'd had a fight with some guy earlier, according to his friends, but he seemed okay. Then he went out to his car to get his cigarettes, and they heard him screaming—by the time they got outside, he was lying there choking to death."

"That's terrible," Cody gulped. "Does it say anything about the guy he was fighting with?"

"Nope. Just his friends say it was some college kid. The bartender said he'd never seen him before. Good thing you were home last night."

"Yeah....." Cody was grateful to Sam but knew it wouldn't stand up. Eventually, his name would get mentioned. He didn't even consider the dead man might not be the dart player—his dream was too fresh....

He glanced down at the ring on his hand and did a double take, bringing it up level with his eye to look more closely. It wasn't his imagination. A tiny rust-brown drop of blood stained the silver fangs.

It had to be a coincidence. After all, he'd hit the man hard enough to knock out a tooth. The blood must have come from the blow...and yet...the teasing memory of the dream replayed in his head—and the satisfaction he had felt.

"Cody, what's wrong? You don't look so hot."

"I don't feel so good. Maybe I'm coming down with something. Uh...listen—I think I'd better go back to bed. Maybe I can stave it off before things get worse."

"But your paper—"

"It's gonna be okay, Mary Ann. You'll see. But I really need to sleep."

Mary Ann gathered her things slowly, her eyes clouded with hurt. "Sure, Cody. Whatever you say."

He practically pushed her out the door. He had a lot to think about.

As soon as he was certain she'd left, Cody grabbed the newspaper and read the entire story for himself. It was too amazing. He had wanted to kill the guy—and now the man had dropped dead. The coincidence was too great. There must be a connection.

He glanced down at the ring once more, and a grin blossomed on his face. If he was right about this…. Only one way to find out.

"All right, Mr. High-and-Mighty Professor. Let's see how you grade this!" He lay back on the couch. "Okay, you little beauty—do your stuff." He closed his eyes and focused his thoughts on Professor Warner, and how much he hated the man. It wasn't just this paper. Warner seemed to delight in making him feel inferior, belittling him in class every chance he got. Well, Cody Eilers was inferior to *no* man, and he would prove it…. Before he could clarify things further in his mind, Cody fell fast asleep.

The next time he woke, golden beams of late afternoon sunlight flooded the room. He glanced down at the ring. Was it his imagination, or was the serpent's hood just a trifle more pronounced? The sapphire eyes glittered in the rays of the sinking sun. It appeared to be smirking at him, and a thrill of fear shuddered up his spine.

He had to know. Grabbing his keys, he headed for the student union. If there *had* been an "accident," it would be the talk of the campus. The

24

rumor mill would grind out speculations even if the body wasn't yet cold....

Students filled the Union that Saturday evening and Cody wove his way through the tables, looking for a place to sit.

"Hey, Eilers!" called a classmate from Film Editing, "did you hear about your favorite Prof.? Seems ol' Doc Warner choked on a chicken bone at lunch—or maybe he just reread your paper...."

"What do you mean?" Cody asked, tone innocent.

"He 'cashed his chips,' 'bought the farm,' and 'planted daisies'—*if* you catch my drift."

"Not really."

"He's dead, man! D-E-A-D, dead. Looks like you'll get a free Incomplete, you lucky SOB. His class really killed my GPA, no pun intended."

Cody gulped. He'd done it. He'd wanted Warner dead, and the man had died. He glanced down at his hand involuntarily.

"Hey, man—you okay? You look a little green."

Cody looked over at the other in panic. "Uh...yeah. I think I'm coming down with something. I've been zonked out all day."

"Well, maybe you ought to go back to bed, friend. You look awful."

"I'll be okay. Uh, listen, have you seen Mary Ann Griffith around here?"

"I think I saw her over near the snack bar about an hour ago, but I doubt she's still there. She was talking to Tyler Armstrong, and it sounded like they were about to head out somewhere."

Cody felt his blood pressure rise. That hadn't taken long. And she didn't even have the courtesy to break up with him? Who did she think she was? "Look, man, thanks. I gotta go."

Cody pushed his way back across the crowded room to the snack bar. Mary Ann sat at a table, laughing up at the sandy-haired Tyler. As Cody walked up, she asked, "When do you want to go?"

"How 'bout 7:00?" Tyler replied.

"Great. I'll be ready…." She caught sight of Cody's glowered face and paled. "Uh, hi, Cody. I thought you were sick."

"Is that why you were making a date with Tyler?"

"Hey—look, Cody, man," Tyler protested, "we're just going to see a film for a class. It's not a date."

"Stay out of this." Cody's fist clenched and unclenched subconsciously.

Tyler's eyes narrowed, focusing on that rhythmic movement. "Take it easy, Cody. You're reading something into this that isn't there."

Cody pushed him away. "Just get out of here— and leave my girl alone."

Mary Ann stood, her chair skittering backward along the tile floor. The sound fell like thunder in the suddenly quiet Union. A snapping fire filled her eyes Cody had never seen before. She was always so placid and pliable…but every camel had its maximum load, and he had finally found the limit to her patience and understanding.

"That does it, Cody Eilers! I am sick and tired of this nonsense! You treat me like dirt. You barely even acknowledge my existence unless it suits your purpose or you want something, and yet when I want to go to a harmless movie with a friend, I'm suddenly 'your girl!' Well, I have news for you, sweetheart. I am not 'your girl.' I am perfectly free to go where and with whom I please. Since you seem unable to grasp that fact, maybe you'd better take this back."

She jerked his promise ring from her finger and threw it at him. "Choke on it! Come on, Tyler. We'll get something to eat before the show." She slipped her arm through Tyler's and led him toward the exit with a furious glance over her shoulder at Cody.

Cody was so incensed he couldn't move. The rage paralyzed him, allowing him only the pulsing contraction of his left hand, and a tremor shivering through him like a convulsion. How dare she? Who did she think she was? The little nobody!

It took several minutes before he could force his feet to move. He strode back to the Mustang and jammed the key into the lock. As usual, he had difficulty getting the car to start, but the delay did nothing to diffuse his anger. The fury filled him like viscous lava bubbling toward eruption.

When the starter finally caught, he floored the accelerator all the way home. At the complex, he stalked inside the apartment, pacing up and down the living room until he finally reined the anger into a malleable ball of hatred. He shaped it, defined it, honed it like a dagger, and slashed his heart in two with it. Ripping photos off the wall, he tore Mary Ann's face into tiny bits. He smashed mementos she had given him, gutted a stuffed elephant, and burned letters….

By nightfall, the apartment was a shambles. Slinging himself down on the couch, with his arm flung over his eyes once more, he fought to calm his breathing. The destruction had dulled the edge of his hatred, but it still flickered inside him. His eyes fluttered closed with a last flare of anger.

Damn Mary Ann! Tyler Armstrong…? She would dump him for Tyler Armstrong? Well, he'd show *her*—wouldn't *she* be sorry? It'd serve her right…. He drifted off to sleep.

The jangling of the telephone jerked him awake. He could have been asleep for minutes or for hours. Cody sat up and reached for the telephone, then froze, staring down at his hand in horror. The ring was gone.

What had he been thinking…? He couldn't remember exactly—his mind stuttered between panic and paralysis. What *had* he been thinking? Something about Mary Ann, and Tyler…a sweep of jealousy and a "wouldn't it serve her right if…?" He hadn't even finished the sentence in his head, but it must have been enough. The mere brush of the thought had unleashed the snake. It was on its way to Mary Ann's!

He bolted from the apartment, not even stopping to lock the door. Her building was only two blocks away—he sprinted the distance rather than waste time coaxing the Mustang. Skidding up to the door of her apartment, he banged loudly and insistently on the panel.

"W-Who is it?" came a soft, tentative call from inside.

"Mary Ann? Thank God. It's me, Cody. Open the door!"

"Cody!" The relief in her voice told him the whole story. "Help me...*please!*"

"The door—"

"I-I can't get there..." she sobbed.

Cody slammed his shoulder into the door, easily splintering the cheap frame. The panel flew open, and he spilled into the living room. He just caught himself before tumbling to the floor and drew in his breath with a hiss as he took in the situation.

Mary Ann cowered against the far wall of the room, clutching a sofa cushion for defense. Her eyes were wide with terror, focusing unblinkingly on the mamba on the other side of the couch.

The serpent stood poised to strike; its head a good six feet from the floor as it reared up, weaving slightly to maintain its balance. The terrified girl huddled well within its strike zone. As Cody crashed into the apartment, the graceful neck swiveled in his direction, and now he found himself mesmerized by the glowing stare of the snake.

He tore his eyes from it, looking for some kind of weapon. Something he could use to kill the snake. He had to destroy it before it hurt Mary Ann. He couldn't let anything happen to her. Not for his stupid jealousy.

Mary Ann whimpered, then darted a hand to her mouth as if to force the sound back down her throat. The creature grew even taller as it reared its head back to strike, its wicked fangs glinting in the light of the chandelier.

"No!" Cody shouted, distracting the snake for a split second. It half turned toward him.

Without conscious thought, Cody launched himself into the room. An intense flare of agony ripped through his whole body as the serpent's fangs sank home in his side. His leap carried him onward; to slam into the floor as the snake dissolved into black mist. It had fulfilled its mission.

"Cody!" Mary Ann screamed, throwing the cushion aside and dropping to her knees beside him. She cradled his head in her lap, tears streaming down her face. "Should I call 911?"

He shook his head weakly. "They wouldn't make it in time," he whispered, raising a shaking hand to brush back her hair.

"Oh, Cody…what can I do?"

"J-just hold me. It should be quick…."

"Cody, I can't just sit here and watch you die!"

"Please…Mary Ann…this way, the snake won't hurt anyone else." He grimaced at a brief spasm of pain.

"What will I do…after?"

"T-tell them I had some kind of attack—they won't expect you to know what it was. S-say it was t-too quick for you to get help. I d-doubt they'll be able to tell what h-happened if they don't know w-what to look for…." He fought for a deep breath. "I-I'm so sorry, Mary Ann. I c-couldn't let it—"

"Shh…," she admonished, placing a finger to his lips. "Lie still. Maybe if you don't talk, the poison won't spread as fast. I'm going to make that call."

She slid a cushion beneath his head and started to rise, but he caught her hand. "No! Don't...Don't you see? M-my thoughts control the snake. All I have to do is think about something happening t-to someone and the snake will kill them. I'm already responsible for two deaths. L-let it end here." He gasped against the growing constriction in his chest, fighting for one more breath. "I l-love you, Mary—"

Cody's eyes closed, and he conceded the fight.

***

In a crowded, dimly lit shop somewhere in the maze of streets making up Chinatown, a small ring box of black velvet caught a stray shaft of light. Smooth, ageless hands straightened the box, and the sunbeam sparked fire from the sapphire eyes of a silver snake.

31

Sin and Revenge (Olivia Arieti)

Nothing more ironic for Sam than finding himself in his boat with his victim's ashes, all pressed in a bottle shaped urn waiting to be scattered in the sea. Never would he have imagined such an epilogue.

"You shouldn't have done that, you bloody asshole," he cried as he steered away from the shore and cursed the remains.

Sam didn't make much money, his boat was old and couldn't venture too far from the coast, so scattering ashes was sort of a second job. Although the area wasn't too populated, the few fishermen there, after a lifelong at sea, frequently wanted their remains thrown into its blue rather than buried in the cold earth.

The village was poor, isolated on a stretch of coast towered by jagged cliffs and surrounded by unspoilt nature. At night time, its raw setting was disquieting. Many swore the souls of the sailors that had found their demise in the waters opposite it, would come out and haunt the terrifying precipices. Most of the houses crowded the main street where a few shops stood longing for the scarce customers. The centenary pub only seemed alive, a hustle and bustle of chattering, drinking and cursing, the refuge of the tired, the lonely and of the lost as well.

Sam had always lived in his thatched cottage with Cathleen, his sister. He had been a father to her, since their parents died prematurely.

The girl blossomed early and her lovely features didn't go unnoticed. Harry, one of the local lads, fell madly in love with her and most ambitious, wanted to offer the best to his bride to be.

Early one morning, the sobbing Cathleen saluted him at the station; her fiancé was on his way to the city sure to find advantageous opportunities for a better future.

Also there though, expectations were hard to fulfil; more than a year had passed and he wasn't ready for the girl's arrival yet.

The days were long for her, alone and distant from her beloved; after tidying up, she would take long walks along the seaside and cast wistful glances at the horizon as if her sweetheart would come back on a splendid liner.

The nights were endless too, black and silent, deprived of whatever promise of a brighter day.

Such a disposition made her an easy prey for the dissolute Edwin. Already in his forties, after years of gambling and heavy drinking, the penniless fellow had to accept his brother's offer to work on the family farm. Vice hadn't altered his features though, and the few streaks of grey hair conferred him a mature and assuring aspect that highly increased his charm.

"Are you a mermaid or a selfie?" he muttered as she passed by him.

"Neither, Sir, just a lonely girl taking a stroll."

"Thank goodness you're for real then," he smiled. "Edwin here, just came back a few days ago after ten years abroad."

"You must be Tom's brother, Sam told me about you."

"Hope he also warned you," he chuckled, 'that I'm not a nice guy."

"If you really were, you wouldn't say so."

"Say, I think I'll like you, doll. If we had had our bathing suits along, I would have suggested going for a swim, it's such a hot afternoon."

Cathleen wondered if her desire to take that swim showed on her face.

Maybe, it did since he added, "I'm sure you want it too, but I know that for a village girl it would be considered inappropriate to go without."

"I presume city girls are rather shameless," she replied.

"Open-minded sounds better. That's why I've always loved dating them."

'What the nerve,' thought Cathleen and was about to speak her mind when he put his finger on her lips, gazed deep in her eyes and sneered, "Don't worry, hon, I'll give you all the time you need to free yourself of those prudish inhibitions and show me the true woman you are."

That said, he saluted her with a sly smile and headed away without ever turning his head.

Cathleen's cheeks were on fire; the fellow's scorn was disturbing, his provocation though, had woken her dormant senses.

That same evening, Sam said, "I'm sorry Edwin's back, he always gets in trouble and gets folks in trouble as well, totally different from his brother, a truly good chap."

Without any comments, Cathleen rushed to her room prey of an unfamiliar itch; the stranger's image had already replaced Harry's one.

Nothing pleased her more than finding him on the beach the following day.

"I'm glad to have the chance to apologise for my straightforwardness, dear," he muttered and took her hand gently, "Will you forgive me?"

She smiled and let him hold her hand.

They walked along the shore and he told her about his life in the city, of his restless past and of his plans for the future that would see a totally changed fellow. It sounded something between a confession and a promise, almost a vow.

"Tom told me you're engaged..." here he paused and shook his head in disapproval, "If I had been your fiancé, I'd never have left such a gorgeous lass behind."

His words struck a chord in Cathleen's heart and for the first time she felt abandoned, neglected. What was taking Harry so long to get back to her?

"What about going for that swim tomorrow?" Edwin said, "got to while away the time somehow..."

Although both brought their swimming suits along, neither used them. Once in the water, Edwin took her in his arms and let his hand run down her back while he kissed her wet face and dripping hair.

When they came out, the bleak cliffs had turned golden hit by the blazing sun, and the sandy carpet was as burning as their passion finally unleashed in the most lascivious embrace.

Time passed quickly now as one encounter followed the other, all in solitary and distant places.

Edwin had totally mesmerised Cathleen and she wanted to be with him forever.

She also had to tell him about the child she was expecting.

They could elope and get away from that grim village that had nothing to offer except rumours and poverty.

"Fatherhood is not for me, sweetie, neither tying whatever knot," the fellow remarked dryly, "Besides, I've never made any promises of that sort."

He snarled, "Maybe, you were right, I'm a nice guy after all."

She stared at him incredulous, as each word stabbed her heart.

"I'm leaving for good, can't stand working on the farm any longer," he concluded and walked away visibly annoyed by her disconsolate glance.

Despair turned into terror, while guilt and regret finally made their way through.

Jumping off the highest cliff was her only way of ending such a torture; the barren crag, as steep as slippery, was waiting for her.

***

Sam found his sister's farewell letter and learned the whole truth only after her burial.

Tears mingled with imprecations, grief with hatred and revenge sprouted in his soul like a malefic weed.

Night after night, he contemplated the blade of his sharpest knife and relished polishing it in order to make it as lucent as possible when penetrating the rogue's heart.

On the evening before Edwin's departure, they met on the same fatal cliff.

"You abominable monster," he shouted, "you're responsible for my sister's death and you'll pay for that."

"What bitch are you talking about?" Edwin sneered.

Flushed with anger, he pushed him towards the edge and struck him so violently that the fellow vacillated, lost his balance and plummeted down. He died on the spot.

For a long while, Sam stood gazing at the body lying feet below. He regretted not having the chance to use his knife. Watching the blood spurting out of the knave's heart would have been better.

The night was pitch black, no moon, no stars, neither the feeble light of a ship gleamed in the distance nor the foam of the waves was visible. The place was deserted, abandoned by all mortals and also by the souls of the drowned sailors.

The hope that crows always on the lookout for carrion would scavenge the hideous flesh accompanied him home.

The corpse was found the following morning. The dynamic of the murder or accident hadn't been easy to solve as many were Edwin's foes and creditors and consequently, many the suspects.

Naturally, not a tear was shed, not even by his brother, who wanted however, to respect his sibling's will to have his ashes scattered in the water before his hometown.

Once enclosed in the urn, Tom went out to fetch his friend.

A refusal might have caused suspicions and after clenching his teeth and another good dose of curses, the fisherman consented to carry out the abhorred wish.

And now, far away from the coast, Sam kept gazing at the bottle.

What if he didn't free the ashes? Dooming them to eternal captivity would have been more satisfying than the lethal strike. The thought of the diabolic villain entrapped at last, made him burst into a loud laughter.

At once, the urn began oscillating and the boat listed badly to the starboard side.

For sure, Edwin's spectre was inside…

Hurriedly, Sam snatched the bottle and scattered the ashes, his hands trembling, his feet doing their best to stick to the shaking floor boards.

Immediately, the brusque movement stopped and everything was still again.

"So that's what you wanted, you've read my mind, bastard," he cried, "too bad sharks don't feed on ashes, for you deserve nothing else."

That said, he steered back to the village.

On the pier stood Cathleen, translucent as ever.

Tears mingled with the bitter brine still on his face; when his eyes were no longer blurred, they beheld the most horrifying blackness.

The Minute Thief (Jackk N. Killington)

Her name was Confetti. Well, her actual name was Connie, but I liked to call her Confetti, because she was always a good time to be with, and hang out with. She wouldn't think twice of either one night showing up with a game of backgammon to play, or another night showing up blasted out of her mind with a stick of butter on her head and holding three cats in her hands. She was spontaneous. She was amazing and I loved the hell out of her.

I met her one night at a Cabonzo show. The band was playing old Misfits songs, but tech-coring them. The bass was violent, and so was the crowd. I got a tooth chipped by a bottle to the cheek while I was flailing in the pit, and Connie was the one that picked me up. She took me to an all-night dentist to have my mouth fixed, and paid for it. I found out later that she was the one that winged the bottle. She was actually aiming for Garr, her ex-boyfriend, and clocked me instead. She felt bad about it, plus her parents were rich so no real cost there.

Anyway, so after that we went out and I watched her eat a pretzel while we sat and talked the rest of the night. It was the most fun that I ever had just talking to someone, in my entire life. She was beautiful. She was fantastic, and after that night, she was also my girlfriend. We started dating and after about three months, we started living together.

Confetti had her own apartment on West Main next to a park, but also next to a dilapidated apartment complex that was haphazardly used for gigs, practice, and living areas for local bands. Considering the only people that lived there were wino's and crack heads, no one cared. Well, they lived there at first but the bands drove them out. Even the homeless had standards it would seem. The Wretcheds Apartment Cohabitation Collaboration, WACC for our own personal shits and giggles, was a great place for our drug and alcohol infused minds to find great music, great friends and the occasional thirds for the night when Confetti wanted to spice things up. Basically, the experience was amazing and I was happy as a clam for the first ten months. After that I kind of fell into a personal hell.

At first it was small things. A PEZ dispenser that I truly liked and kept around so I could flick its empty head back and forth. Donald duck had to pay for his war crimes, don't you know? But then, a video game here, a CD there. It was stuff that I figure I probably lost along the way, left at a Circle K or a Taco bell lobby, or a friend's house. I never really had a problem with the loss of the stuff that just wound up going missing. I just chocked it up mostly to my own error or a couple punk klepto friends that were known to be handsy with other people's shit. If you have a group of friends in your twenties, you've probably had a few of these assholes that you continued to let hang out with you, even though you knew they were ripping you off, but they were either fun to hang with, look at, or fuck, so you never really minded all that much, but yeah, small things disappeared and were gone from my life, and after a short time, I forgot that they even existed. That is, at least until my father disappeared.

Just as the old saying went, my dad went out for a gallon of milk one night and just never came back. You heard about that happening from time to time, but always about the guy who finds out that the wife is pregnant. Never the forty-seven-year-old man with a three count of kids that he had already raised and gotten out the door and into their own lives. One grand-kid already on the way.

My mother was heartbroken. What could have brought this on? Was he dead somewhere? They never even found the car either. A nineteen ninety-eight Buick LeSabre that my dad loved. Did he spontaneously go gay? Was he wearing a dress and calling himself Rolletta? His name was Rolland. Was he living his best life now in Albuquerque? We had no way of knowing.

My mom called the cops, obviously, and they treated it like a joke, because that is what cops do. They took my mom's name and info and said that they would get back to her if any information or if a body turned up. They said that to her. Our nation's finest, and that was it for Rolland. We never saw him again, or the LeSabre. He just poofed out of the world and out of our lives.

For a few weeks my mother was inconsolable, answering the phone at a run, hoping that it would either be Rolland or the cops saying that they found him in the best or worst case scenario. After a few weeks though, she seemed to stop worrying about him, and then she never mentioned him. One day me and Confetti were at her house and I asked her how she was holding up. "About what?" she asked.

"About dad?" I said.

"Who?" she asked.

"Dad? Rolland? Your husband. My dad? Fran and Jake's dad?"

Her face was cold. There was no humor or sarcasm in her voice or demeanor. "I have absolutely no idea who you are talking about. Why the fuck would I marry someone named Rolland." She visibly shuddered at the name.

"Explain us?" I said.

My mom looked kind of spaced out for a moment, as if she were searching for a thought. Then she smiled. "I had all three of you with IVS. I never found a guy I wanted to take the condom off for, so I just had you guys."

"How?" I asked. "You've never worked a day in my life. How did you get the house, any of it?

Again, she went quiet, but it was different this time. She kept looking inside of herself, and the harder that she looked, the more stressed out she was. The more sad that she got. Then she started to convulse. Falling to the ground and shaking. My mom did not have seizures, but I knew something was very wrong with her by that point. I called the ambulance, and they showed up a few minutes later. They were able to get my mother under control and get her into the ambulance. I didn't know then, but that was the last time that I would ever see her.

After I watched them close the door and found out where they were taking her. I watched them pull away and went back in the house. I closed the door behind me and went into the kitchen. Fran and Jake had to know, I thought as I picked up my cell from the counter. I scrolled through my contacts and hit Jake's number. He let it go to voice mail. I hung up and tried again. I did this two more times before the person picked up the phone. "The fuck do you want? It's eight goddamn thirty."

"Jake?" I asked.

"There's no Jake here. You've got the wrong number." The person on the other end of the line hung up.

"That's weird," I said.

"What?" Confetti asked.

"Jake must have changed his number and not told me." I was confused, but it wouldn't be the first time that one of us had had a brain fart and forgot to tell anyone that they lost their phones and had to change numbers. It happens. Hopefully Fran would know. So I called her.

"Hello?" Fran answered the phone after the second ring.

"Hey Fran. This is Luke. Mom just got sent..."

"Who?" Fran said. She sounded genuinely confused.

"Don't fuck around," I said. I was not in the mood to play. "This is Luke. I'm calling because mom..."

"I don't know a Luke, and don't you get all dicky on me, I don't know who you are. How do

43

you know me? You some fucking psycho or something?"

"What the fuck is going on?" I whispered. "Look, I don't know what is going on, but mom just got sent to the hospital."

"I don't have a mom; I was an orphan since I was born. Look this really hurts me. Don't call me again you fucking prick." Then Fran hung up the phone.

I put down the phone, and just kind of stared at it for a bit. "What's wrong?" Confetti asked me from the other side of the counter.

"I don't know." I started to cry. I didn't know what to do, so I just stood there and I cried. I felt like I was losing my mind.

Confetti walked around the counter and hugged me as I let it out. "Why don't we get you to the hospital and see your mom? Once we know that she's okay we can move on from there. Okay?" Confetti asked. How she was my rock at that time. I absolutely fell in love with her a little at that moment.

"Yeah, okay," I said, and let her lead me out to the car. It was a quiet ride to the hospital, with me looking out the window for the most part and Confetti concentrating on the driving. Driving in the city was always bad, but tonight it seemed like everybody was driving like an idiot so she needed the extra attention and I needed the extra quiet time to think, so that's how we went to Robertson Memorial.

When we got there we walked up to the emergency reception area. "Hi," I said to the pretty

44

looking woman behind the counter. "My mother was just brought in. Madison Alunon?" I asked.

The receptionist punched up a few screens on her computer and after a moment she closed them and looked at me. "There is no record of a woman coming here with that name. Do you have an address?" I gave her the address. "No, I'm sorry, but there is no one from that address here right now or on route."

"Well, I watched one of your ambulances pull out of my mom's parking lot. There was a guy and a woman. Kevin and Lisa I think were their names."

"We do have two EMS drivers with those names, but they've been in the break room eating a pizza for the last forty-five minutes. Would you like to speak with them?"

"Yeah, sure," I said as the receptionist picked up the phone and paged them. I gave a worried look to Confetti as we waited.

Kevin and Lisa showed up five minutes later. They were the same people that picked up my mom. I asked them about her. "Nope. Never got that run tonight," Lisa said, Kevin nodded his head.

"Oh come the fuck on," I partially yelled in frustration and part from fear. "I watched you, the both of you, load up my mom in the goddamn ambulance not more than a half hour ago. This is bullshit," I yelled. "Where the fuck is my mom?"

I was pissed. I felt like everyone, including my own family was playing some kind of colossal mind fuck on me. The woman behind the counter looked pissed and she picked up the phone, probably calling security. The other two, Kevin, and Lisa just kind of went rigid in front of me. Not scared. Not in anger. They looked like they were trying to remember, and it was the same look that happened right before…

"We need to go," Confetti said as Kevin and Lisa started to foam at the mouth and fell to the ground in convulsions. Confetti was pulling on my arm now, as security ran into the room, but instead of going after me and Confetti, they ran to Kevin and Lisa as they shook. "Luke, we have to go." She started to pull harder and I gave up, letting her half drag me through the sliding double doors of the emergency room. Before long I was back in her car and riding down the streets back to her place. I was understandably quiet and so was she. I figured that we would talk when we got home, and we did.

"Look, we'll start calling the hospitals. She's got to be somewhere," Confetti said. I felt emotionally rung out. I tried Fran and Jake again. Fran did not answer, and the guy who answered the first time was even more belligerent the second. Said something about a frying pan full of bacon grease and my asshole. I decided to let that go for the night. So we called all of the hospitals in the city. Not some of them. All of them.

We got nothing. No one in the city had her name on file as being there, ever, so we called the police. There was no record of a call to 911. Then they said something that was even weirder. "There was no house at 3343 Marigold Lane," the cop said that there was no record of a house ever being there.

"That's impossible," I yelled into the phone.

"It is what it is," the officer on the end of the line said without emotion or compassion. Then he started talking about mental health clinics in the area and how they might be able to help me. That's when I hung up.

"I cannot believe this bullshit," I said as I sat on the couch and rubbed my head and face. I didn't know what to do. It was as if everyone, including Fran, had forgotten who I was. Our mom. Probably our dad. "I don't know what to do," I said to Confetti who sat next to me as the TV droned on about the next best sitcom that was pretty much an amalgamation of every other show that they had on their lineup. I wasn't listening. TV was bullshit anyway. I flipped on music instead.

"We'll figure it out in the morning babe," Confetti said, kissing me.

"Yeah, I guess we will." I looked at the clock. It was four AM. Already morning, and no solutions, but I was tired. Bone tired. We fell asleep on the couch, holding each other.

***#

"Wake up sleepy head," I heard Confetti call me away from my sleep. I woke up with her straddling me. My mouth was open. Tendrils of light were flowing from my mouth to hers. I didn't know what it was. Didn't know what it meant, but as I sat there. I didn't know what anything was anymore. She smiled when I opened my eyes, purring. "Good morning little sunshine."

I looked around the room, but I didn't remember anything, didn't remember who she was. Worst of all, I couldn't remember who I was. She

47

made me write all this down actually. She liked to keep a memoir of her victims. Confetti always did like a party.

I stared at her for a moment and then I looked past her at the TV. I saw my reflection in the screen. I felt like I was at least twenty years older. I don't know how I even remembered that much, but I could have sworn that when I fell asleep I was in my twenties, but was I? Who am I? I asked myself and then she looked me in the eyes. "What is your name?" she asked.

I looked at my reflection and then back at her. Confetti seemed to be a little younger looking then she had yesterday. I knew the answer before I opened my mouth, and she smiled at my answer. "I am food."

Welcome to Deer Country (Jason R Frei)

Earl leaned his shoulder unsteadily against the deer blind. He giggled to himself as he unzipped his pants and tried to write his name in the snow. Moonlight shone through the trees, casting him as a dark shadow against the white background. He finished his John HandCock (he laughed out loud at this, like a short bark in the silent night), zipped up and stumbled back inside. Crushed and empty beer cans littered the floor of the blind.

"You are way too loud," said Homer. "You're gonna scare away all the deer."

Earl popped the tab on another can of silver bullet. "We've been here for three hours and haven't seen shit yet."

Homer opened his mouth to respond when the snapping of a twig caused them both to freeze. Earl slowly set down his can and picked up his rifle. His friend tiptoed to the far side of the blind and picked up his as well. They met in the middle of the window and scanned the area in front of them.

"Over there." Homer pointed to a large, dense bush a few yards in front of them. A pair of antlers stuck up from the foliage.

Earl aimed his gun, his finger tense on the trigger. After a moment, he lowered the weapon.

"You'll need to do it," he said to Homer. "I drank too much and I'm seeing double."

Homer patted him on the shoulder and then raised his rifle. He looked down the sight and grunted.

"The bush is too thick to see what I'm shooting at."

"Aim at the antler to your right and then drop your barrel down about two feet."

The hunter aimed his Remington at the right antler, dropped the barrel and looked hard through the scope. He barely saw some tawny between the green leaves and covering of snow. He took a breath in, steadied his hands and squeezed the trigger.

The shot echoed in the woods, scattering birds in all directions from the treetops. Both men saw the antlers buck up once and then disappear behind the brambles. Silently, they left the blind and approached the hopeful kill site.

Earl rounded the bush and stopped dead in his tracks, so abruptly that Homer ran into him. Laid out on the ground before them was a creature that neither had ever seen. In fact, it was a creature that should not exist. Tawny fur covered a torso that was thick around the middle. Its arms and legs were fairly thin and also covered in coarse tawny fur. Sharp black hooves terminated at the end of the legs. The hands though, were three-fingered. Thick black nails jutted from the ends of the fingers like normal fingernails. Its head was roughly human shaped and contained humanoid eyes, a mouth and a nose. The eyes were a deep chocolate brown with a large dark pupil in the middle. Felt-covered antlers, beautiful sixteen-pointers, sprouted from the forehead above the liquid eyes. Long tapered ears, rimmed in black, stuck out from the sides of the head. Blood oozed from a puckered hole in its chest.

"What the hell is that?" asked Earl.

Homer turned away and vomited. Cold sweat ran down the sides of his face. Tremors coursed through his body. When the heaving subsided, he stood up and wiped his mouth with the sleeve of his coat. A branch snapped loudly in the forest, like another gunshot going off. Both men raised their guns with shaky hands.

Noises rose up around them—more branches snapping, iced snow crunching, grunting. The birds had gone silent.

"Let's get out of here," whispered Earl.

Neither man made to move until a deep-throated scream sounded off to their right. The sound spurred them into action. Earl and Homer turned and ran, going in opposite directions. Crashing sounds came from behind them, as well as other odd vocalizations.

Earl ran back to the deer blind, sheer panic urging him on. He was almost to the door when a massive dark shape barreled into him. He flew sidelong into a tree, knocking his head hard. He got to his feet, blinking rapidly to clear his blurred vision.

Earl screamed as the shape turned on him. The creature was the size of a bear. A massive rack of antlers twisted out of its immense head. Powerful arms, covered in thick fur, reached for him. Earl saw dirt under the black claws of its three-fingered hand. He swung his rifle at the approaching monster, feeling the butt end of the gun hitting something solid and meaty. Without a second thought, he turned and sprinted off into the forest.

The moon slashed the snow-covered forest floor as Earl ran. He was afraid that, at any moment, another creature would pounce from the shadows. He crested a small hill and slid down the other side, finding himself in a gully filled with waist deep snow. His panic surged.

Another small hill loomed in front of him and he half ran, half swam through the cold snow. He climbed the hill, panting and crying. At the top, he scanned the trees while catching his breath and saw that he was alone.

He laughed to himself, small clouds blowing out from his mouth. Slender threads of snow snaked down his pant legs. Earl turned and walked three steps before a slim wire hooked around his ankle and yanked him upside down in the air. The Winchester fell from his grasp and sunk into the snow. He spun slowly around like a ballerina on a silk rope. Blood rushed to his head and he could hear it crashing in his ears.

Strong hands gripped him from behind. He twisted around to face the behemoth that had pursued him. He opened his mouth to scream and caught a woolly fist hard to his teeth. The scream died behind his mashed and bloody lips. Liquid brown eyes looked down at him. Moonlight glinted off a blade held in its mutated hand.

The creature sneered and drove the knife into Earl's stomach. The cold of the winter air and of the blade drove the breath from his lungs. With a tearing sound, the knife slid down and opened Earl from his groin to his gullet. Bright splashes of crimson blood marred the pristine white ground. The last thing he saw were his steaming intestines loop past his eyes.

Homer zigzagged through the dense trees, slipping and sliding on the frozen earth. A doe jumped into his path and he slid to a halt, landing on his butt. The deer spooked and ran off. The man jumped to his feet and felt something grab the back of his hunting jacket. He reeled around and fired a shot waist high. A thin cervine creature grunted and fell.

The woods came alive with the sounds of grunting and screaming. Homer spun around, wide-eyed and shot at anything that moved. Another creature stepped into view. Homer pulled the trigger and the hammer dropped down on an empty chamber. He threw the rifle and ran.

More creatures bounded after him. He saw the shapes to his left and right. Some ran on twos, like a human, while others ran on all fours. He spotted the edge of the woods and made a break for it.

The moon shone silver on the clearing ahead and Homer saw the awaiting pickup truck. He was halfway to the truck when he stopped. He rubbed his eyes and looked again. Earl's gutted body was strapped to the hood like a trophy. Blood dripped down the sides of the white front fenders, creating pools of scarlet in the snow.

An immense deer-like creature rose from behind the truck and walked toward him. Homer turned to find other creatures emerging from the woods. They came in all shapes, colors and sizes, but they shared similar cervine traits—large brown eyes, black hooved feet, and brownish fur.

Homer dropped to his knees and pleaded for his life.

"Please," he said between sobs. "We didn't know."

A crumpled beer can pelted him in the side of the head. A slim trickle of blood slid down his cheek, mixing with the tears and snot. A strong broad leg kicked him in the back, throwing him prone to the ground. He screamed for his life as the herd gathered around him, but it was cut short as dozens of legs stomped down on his defenseless body. Blood mixed with snow, creating a frothy churned mess. When they finished, the herd slipped back into the forest to bury their own.

Trapped (Ian McKinley)

I slammed the basement door closed behind me and managed to push a bolt into place before a heavy body crashed into it. The three youths had been raping a young woman in an alleyway when I spotted the attack and rashly charged forward, shouting at them to release the girl. I hoped that they would run off, but they simply turned to face me, clearly very annoyed at my interruption. This was Glasgow, so no guns: just razors and knives. I immediately took to my heels and the trio raced after me, but not before slashing the woman's throat.

I wiped sweat from my face and examined the door in more detail. It was metal-clad and seemed strong enough, but the single bolt was cheaply made and already beginning to buckle from the barrage of blows. I might be secure for a little time, but my pursuers were not going to give up: I had seen their faces and could certainly identify them.

The room was dimly lit by the watery Scottish twilight penetrating a couple of dirty slit windows. Kicks rained onto the door while I quickly fought through cobwebs to check the windows: both barred and, in any case, leading into a shaft to street level that was way too narrow for my large frame. As my eyes adjusted, I could see that the basement was empty apart from a wooden table and the floor was covered by a thick layer of dust. No likelihood of anyone just popping down here to check what was going on.

I hefted the table, but it was too light to provide a suitable barrier in the absence of some way of bracing it against the door. Nevertheless, lifting it caused a sound, so I turned it around to reveal a closed drawer. It was locked, but the lock burst as soon as I wrenched on it, although it jammed only partially open. I groped within and cursed when the contents were revealed: a large, heavy crucifix and squeeze bottle labelled *holy water*. It seemed that someone had been worrying about the undead, but these weapons would do little against my living opponents.

I was beginning to panic, my heart was racing, my hands shaking and I felt warmth indicating that I had pissed myself. Only a dribble and I was thankful for a recently emptied bladder. Strangely, the distraction caused by my fear-induced incontinence helped me calm down. I closed my eyes and forced myself to breathe slowly. I was trapped, but I was sure that there was a way to escape if I could only relax and think it through. I opened my eyes and then noticed a door in a dark corner. My hopes of an easy way out were dashed when I pulled the door open to reveal only a small toilet, again in the light of a slit window leading only to a narrow shaft. Once more I concentrated on slow breathing while I searched for something I could use to defend myself. Nothing at all there except for a plastic bottle that, from the array of warning labels, appeared to contain some kind of concentrated bleach for cleaning drains.

Gradually a possible solution began to emerge. The lines from a comic I had once read came to mind, something about the person who wins a fight not being the strongest, the fastest or the most skilful; but the one who is most prepared to fuck-up his opponents. These guys were making a very big mistake.

I returned to the table and replaced the holy water with the acrid contents of the bleach bottle, careful not to spill any of the foul-smelling fluid. With the squeeze bottle in one hand and the crucifix swinging from the other I returned to the metal door and leant against it. The voices outside were indistinct and in an almost unintelligible local dialect, but the thugs were clearly counting to synchronise their kicks at the door. This was working, as the bolt was almost completely bent loose.

I stood to the side and, on a shout of "ten" from outside, pulled the bolt back just before the door crashed open, causing the youths to stagger forward. Taking advantage of their surprise, I sprayed bleach into eyes of nearest one, who immediately fell onto his knees, screaming in agony. The spray also caught the face of my second attacker, causing him to jump backwards and crash into his companion while he struggled to wipe the irritant away without damaging himself with the Stanley knife he had been brandishing. Due to the bright light in the corridor outside, I had a clear advantage in being able to better see my opponents. The one who had been missed entirely by the bleach was holding a long blade, so I threw the empty bottle at him and, as he twitched to avoid it, scythed the cross down onto his forearm, smashing it and resulting in a gush of blood as bits of bone broke through the skin. "Fucking kill this old bastard," he screamed, just before I kicked him in the groin and he dropped to his knees.

It must have been adrenalin, but everything seemed to happen in slow motion. "Now you shits have got to realise that there are consequences from your actions," I stated in my best pulpit voice while clubbing my first victim on the back of his head. "The politically-correct woke-types worry more about the poor upbringing of rapists and murderers, striving to rehabilitate them while ignoring those who suffer from their predations." I shifted to a two-handed grip on the cross and smashed it into the face of the second thug with so much force that it lifted him from the ground with a loud crack that could have been his neck breaking.

It could also have been the crucifix, as the shaft had snapped and the cross-piece was dangling from it due only to connection via the metal Jesus. I tossed it aside and picked up the long-bladed knife that had been dropped in front of me. "The Old Testament had it right – the *eye for an eye* approach. Castration for rapists and capital punishment for murderers. This definitely ensures no repeat offenders, like the ones who now get put away for a few years in prisons where they live in better conditions than many of our poorer, hard-working citizens."

I grabbed the hair of the rapist with the smashed arm, who was now only semiconscious, and stabbed him several times in the groin. His scream of pain did, however, show that he was aware enough for my purposes. "You're a brutal rapist and, if you were to survive, you're the type that would just do it again." The flow of blood could indicate that his penis and testicles were detached, but caused him to faint in any case. "But you murdered a young girl, so you're not going to survive under any circumstances," I pushed the knife into his eye, jamming it up to the hilt and then wrenching it free and allowing his lifeless body to slump to the floor.

The blinded guy was still screaming, curled in a foetal ball with his face in his hands. I seized one of his feet and dragged him further into the basement, noting that the fly of his jeans was still unzipped. "Well, I hope that you're completely blind as that'll mean an end to your rapes," I stabbed the front of his exposed underpants, "but better safe than sorry." I sawed the blade back and forward to enlarge the wound. "There you go, not a male any more, much less an alpha one." The rapist squealed in agony and was frantically trying to protect both his face and his groin, giving me an opportunity to pull the knife free and slash it across his throat. "Of course, you gratuitously also slashed that poor girl, how do you like that?"

I expected the remaining yob to be dead but, as I moved closer to him, I saw he was slowly choking on the blood and loose teeth that filled his smashed mouth. I vaguely felt that I should have been disturbed by the protruding bits of bone from his caved-in skull, but all I could think of was the terror that must have been experienced by the victim of their rape. I crouched down and took my time to slowly open his belt and the buttons of his ripped jeans. "Well, you're not going to make it, but there's a principle involved. This has to act as a deterrent and I suspect that, for many of your contemporaries, the threat of castration would be more frightened than that of death." While I severed his wedding tackle, I noted that his breathing ceased.

Only when I issued a sigh of relief did I hear the moan from the direction of the door. Standing there, her face ashen, was a heavily built, middle-aged woman in a uniform. At I slowly climbed to my feet, I thought at first that she was a policewoman, but then was relieved to spot that she was actually a traffic warden of some kind.

"Don't come near me," she shouted in a voice that was close to hysteria, waving a phone in my direction. "I'm streaming video of all of this, so just get back!"

"No, you've got this wrong," I pleaded, "These bastards raped and killed a girl and were chasing me. It's them you should be worried about."

"There was a girl assaulted, but I saw her walk to the ambulance. She's certainly not dead."

"But they raped her, slashed her. I saw it and they would have killed me. There were three of them!"

"Three kids," she screamed, tears in her eyes. "Look at them and look at you! How could they hurt you?"

For the first time I looked more carefully at my attackers. They were not only young – fifteen or sixteen, maybe even less – but really skinny. It's not something I'm very conscious of but, as I lift weights about 5 times a week, I'm pretty heavily built. I had actually been returning from the gym when this happened, so was still quite pumped-up. I probably weigh as much as any two of them, with more muscle mass than all three put together. "They had weapons, knives…"

"You're the one with the knife, you sicko! I saw you butchering those defenceless boys."

I dropped the knife as if it was suddenly red hot. "But it wasn't what you think."

"You've got no excuse; I heard you talking to yourself as you did it. You sexually abused them, and must have liked it." She pointed at my groin before turning to the side and vomiting.

Slowly I looked down. There did, indeed, appear to be a bulge in the front of my sweat-suit bottoms. This was maybe exaggerated by the jock strap I was wearing, but I certainly appeared to have a bit of an erection. Then I spotted the damp patch from my earlier loss of bladder control. This did not look at all good.

I heard the sound of running boots on the stairs outside and a shout of "Police!" I had nothing more to say and simply stood with my head hung low. Now I was really trapped and I had no cunning plan that would get me out this time.

Ludo's Portal (Carl Hughes)

Ludo Howard hated his name. The Howard bit was okay and he'd have had no problem with it as a forename either. But *Ludo!* His parents might as well have called him Tiddlywinks or Backgammon. But there it was on his birth certificate and though Mum and Dad said they thought the name noble and dignified, the kids at school ridiculed him to the moon and back. Even the teachers, who should have known better, smirked when they called out his name in class.

What none of them realised was that the boy possessed a special talent – a talent denied to everyone else – and they'd do well not to cross him.

Ludo was three, an age when a child's memories begin to coalesce and imagination takes root, when his power first emerged.

He was kneeling on the rug, playing with a toy that jangled and lit up, while Mum and Grandma Pearson were talking about rip-off supposed bargains on eBay. The TV set was standing in the corner muttering to itself: stuff concerning antiques and cash in the attic. The women's conversation was pretty normal, no hint of animus or friction, when Ludo realised as one instant passed into the next that Grandma Pearson was wishing him and his mother dead. Not just dead but gutted and torn to shreds, fit only for feeding to old Mrs Grainger's two Dobermans next door. To a child just emerging from toddlerhood, that came as stern stuff especially as Grandma Pearson had always seemed okay with him, if not affectionate, while she and Mum had seemed to get along as well as most in-laws did.

Grandma Pearson's hatred washed into Ludo's mind like a scummy tide on a polluted beach. He looked up, startled, and saw that though his grandmother was smiling, her face all dimples and rouge, her eyes were cold and as packed with loathing as if it had been stuffed there by a malice machine.

Attentive rather than scared, as curious as any healthy child, Ludo found himself viewing Grandma's mind as easily as if he were watching the talking TV set. And what he saw there scared him. For Grandma Pearson was raving mad.

He knew that Grandma had brought up her son (Ludo's father) entirely on her own, working hard at several cleaning jobs to provide for them both after Grandpa Pearson swanned off with what Mum called a floozie. The trouble was, Grandma hadn't simply provided for Dad – she'd sort of owned him and controlled his whole life. She arranged his friendships, froze out those whom she considered bad influences, and expected him to remain a bachelor, under her thumb, until she finally popped her sweaty clogs. But Dad had met Mum, fallen in love with her and they'd married in spite of Grandma Pearson's screaming threats to kill herself.

Now, Grandma's feelings were murderous. She didn't just resent Mum and Ludo – she *hated* them with such a passion that it hurt her stomach and gave her diarrhoea. She prayed each night for God to kill Mum and Ludo in a car crash or to have them sprayed with gunfire in a drive-by shooting so that she and Dad could live together again, just the two of them. The boy understood all this because he could see it and feel it and it made him queasy.

He also knew, though he didn't understand how, that Grandma Pearson was (unbeknown to her) already suffering from the stomach cancer that would kill her within nine months.

And so it happened.

Mum and Dad were good parents, loving and tolerant towards their mischievous son, and after Grandma Pearson's death the family became more united. It was as if a festering sore had healed.

Ludo knew even before his schooldays began that he could manipulate his parents merely by putting thoughts into their minds. If he wanted an ice cream, something that Mum normally frowned upon as it contained few nutrients, he only had to wish it and Mum would exclaim, 'Tell you what, Ludo – why don't I treat you to a 99er?'

Dad was an equal pushover. He promised to take Ludo to see United play as soon as the boy reached the age of eight. 'Anything less than that's too young,' he declared. But Ludo wanted to go *now*, at four years of age, and he put an intolerable thought into Dad's mind that he was denying the boy a treat to which he had a right and that he, Dad, was a parent of unparalleled evil. Within the hour, Dad fidgeted with bad vibes and said, 'I know, Ludo – let's go see United on Saturday.'

Ludo had great fun making people uncomfortable by staring at the backs of their heads. They squirmed, wriggled, and had to turn around and when they did so they met his brazen gaze.

Even better, he wished an intolerable itch on neighbour Mr Grainger's arse so that the old guy went down the road scratching with abandon while Ludo chortled his young head off. Then when the curmudgeonly Mr Hamer, who hated children on sight, shouted at Ludo for playing noisily outside his house, Ludo gave him such an excruciating pain in the testicles merely by willing it that the old man vomited over his jumper. The boy was enjoying himself immensely.

There were benefits to others from Ludo's gift, too. He first discovered this when Mum had an excruciating migraine, a condition from which she'd suffered all her life. Ludo, aged five, told her to chuck away her pills because he could do a better job. And he did. He traced his fingers gently across Mum's forehead and, presto, the migraine vanished, never to return.

When Mrs Trent down the road hobbled past, crippled by arthritis, Ludo ran up to her and said he could make her better. Smiling despite her pain, Mrs Trent ruffled his hair and said, 'That's very nice of you, Ludo, but I don't think you're quite old enough to be a doctor yet.'

Ludo looked into the elderly woman's face, which was as plain as a bucket, and said, 'Let me touch you and you'll be better – I promise.'

Mrs Trent's expression turned from amusement to vague alarm, as if she'd met a psychopath on a country lane at dusk. But she said, 'All right then, Ludo, you can touch me if you like.'

So Ludo touched her hands and crabby legs and Mrs Trent gasped. She told Ludo's mother afterwards that a warm, tingling sensation coursed through her body and the pain lifted as if the sun had come out on a summer dawn. The woman's arthritis wasn't entirely cured, only alleviated, but it was never as bad in the future. Ludo was still discovering his power, which wouldn't be fully developed for a few years yet.

As he became older, the boy identified another fascinating gift: he could make things disappear. Coins, toys, anything he desired could be despatched into a void that no one else was aware of and for which Ludo as yet had no name. He understood only that with his mind he could open a slight rip in the fabric of reality and send whatever he liked through that gap and into another realm that no one knew about. Later, he learned that the name for that type of opening was a portal. At first it was fun, whizzing neighbour Mrs Whittaker's dentures into the void, and the spectacles of Fanny Thompson at school likewise. And he'd never forget the expression on the face of his least favourite teacher, Mr Grice, when his chalkboard rubber vanished as he was about to pick it up.

Ludo soon realised that the portal could be used for bigger and more useful purposes. By opening it wider, it was possible to despatch those who had bullied or otherwise wronged him. They simply vanished and all searches by police and neighbourhood squads failed to find them.

The first such victim was Michael O'Connor, a muscular, swaggering braggart who despite being only eleven years of age worked out at the gym and was encouraged by his equally arrogant father to prey on those weaker than himself. 'Whatever our Mike wants from weaklings who cross his path, our Mike gets,' said Mr O'Connor proudly, as if boasting of some precious stone found at the bottom of a mine shaft.

Michael O'Connor ridiculed Ludo for his ridiculous name and he ensured that his coterie of sycophantic hangers-on did the same. Worse, he bullied Ludo into providing answers to tricky homework questions and if those answers proved to be wrong, he beat up the smaller boy.

It was after one such beating that Ludo decided that Michael O'Connor had to go. If coins, toys, dentures, spectacles and chalkboard rubbers could be sent through the portal, why not a vicious piece of humanity? It was true that Ludo had previously opened the portal only slightly but he learned quickly that it was no great shakes to make it wide enough to accommodate O'Connor.

The bully's father went on TV to plead for the return of his beloved son, whom he described as 'a gentle soul whom everybody liked', and the police dragged ponds and rivers, raided the homes of known paedophiles, and put tracker dogs on the scent of a boy who would no longer disrupt Ludo's life.

Of course no one ever found a clue as to O'Connor's whereabouts, nor those who in succeeding months and years followed him into what Ludo thought of as *The Great Beyond*. There was no other name for it. What Ludo found slightly alarming, though not a deterrent, was a great bellowing, clamorous uproar as from a horde of immense carnivorous beasts when each of his victims passed from this world into whatever lay beyond the portal. As they entered the portal, those victims screamed and screeched as if they were being torn limb from limb and gutted while still breathing. The boy giggled, smothered in a syrup of glee.

Ludo had read on some obscure web page created in India or Tibet or some other faraway place that those who were dying in agony didn't hear their own screams. He regarded that with contempt. How could anyone in Tibet possibly know what the dead could or couldn't hear in the moments before they passed on? Even God Almighty would be hard pushed to keep track of that sort of knowledge, and in any case Ludo believed in God as much as he believed in leprechauns bludgeoning fairies to death with golden shillelaghs.

When he was fifteen, Ludo became infatuated with a girl called Melanie Bruce who was the same age but so much more sophisticated than he. She inducted him into the joys of sex: an activity that Ludo had previously only read about surreptitiously in the true-life magazines to which his mother subscribed. He found that the real thing was so much more exquisite than the kinky activity described in those magazines by frustrated males who wrote under female pseudonyms.

Blinkhill Park was a green oasis on the edge of town and that was where Ludo and Melanie made out. To Ludo it was excitement on steroids but

68

Melanie complained, 'You come too soon – has any girl ever told you that before?'

'Yeah, well, maybe I just like a quick shag before getting on to the next one,' Ludo told her with an apparent brashness that disguised his chagrin.

Melanie wasn't impressed. Her face drew into a grimace of scorn that Ludo didn't like one bit. In his world, no one had a right to look that way at a guy with his talents. Not that Melanie or anyone else knew about the powers he wielded or how he'd used them. It was Ludo's secret and he intended to nurture his abilities and maybe one day use them to become rich. He hadn't yet decided how that might happen but he had time on his side.

In late October, just before Halloween, Ludo sympathised when Melanie pleaded a headache one night and said she had to stay at home to sleep it off. He could have cured the pain in an instant but he was still smarting from that look of scorn she'd turned on him, so he decided to let her suffer. When she made the same excuse two nights later, and again the following week, he became suspicious.

On the first Tuesday evening in November, which had been a cold day with wind blustering through the stark trees and stripping them of their leaves, Ludo put on his quilted parka, pulled up the hood and ventured into the upmarket estate where Melanie lived with her snobby parents. He took cover in the dense shadows between two lampposts and waited. According to Melanie, she'd developed a migraine.

A few cars passed, BMWs, Mercs and a Jag, but Ludo paid them little heed. He was watching Melanie's house.

He was incensed, but not surprised, when a little after seven o'clock a big Barranca pulled up outside the Bruce house and a dark-haired guy with a lot of bling got out and sauntered up the driveway. Melanie was waiting for him. She opened the door and they embraced, and even from fifty metres away Ludo could hear the peal of her laughter. Then the pair kissed and canoodled and hurried through the wind into the warmth of the bling guy's car.

Ludo felt as if his insides were incendiary, burning and consuming his core. The bitch had cheated on him – he, Ludo, who had power enough to rule the world if he chose. Which meant only one thing: Melanie had to go.

He simmered and brooded all night and paid scant attention to his schoolwork next day. At three-thirty, when the dismissal bell sounded, he approached Melanie and said, 'We've got to talk.'

'Not now, Ludo – I've another headache,' she said.

'Sure you have. But not as big a headache as you're giving me.'

She paused, staring into his face as if it contained the wisdom of lost ages. Then she said, 'Ludo, there's something I have to tell you.'

'No need, I already know. But we don't have to be enemies. Let's go behind the canteen where we'll be alone and can sort things out between us. Then that'll be that.'

The canteen was a cream-painted block detached from the main school buildings. Scrubby growth proliferated and a foul odour arose from the dustbins and cans used for waste food.

Melanie had raven hair and slightly dusky skin, as if she possessed gipsy blood, and perhaps that came with a sixth sense too because once behind the canteen a gleam of alarm showed in her eyes.

'Too late to worry now, Babe,' Ludo said with a smile that could have come from a Hammer horror movie.

His mind got to work instantly. He opened the portal and despatched Melanie through it. From the other side came the voracious, ferocious roaring with which Ludo had become familiar and which never failed to excite him. On entering the portal Melanie screamed and screeched in a way that aroused the boy volcanically, giving him a hard on. She sounded as if she were being disembowelled or torn apart by something as gargantuan as it was obscene. The process took only seconds and then where two people had ventured behind the canteen, only one reappeared.

When Melanie failed to return home from school, her parents called the police and a search was mounted. Appeals went out on TV and radio, posters appeared showing the girl at her smiling best, and Ludo knew it would be only a matter of time before he was approached by the constabulary.

Sure enough, a couple of Plod called at his home. One of them was a man with purple veins in his nose that revealed a passion for whisky or other hard stuff. The other was a wispy woman who

71

blinked too much, as if her contact lenses were causing problems.

'You're Melanie Bruce's boyfriend, we understand,' said the male officer.

'Not really. We went out a few times but agreed to part. No blame on either side,' Ludo said. 'I haven't seen Melanie recently except at school. I think she found a nice boyfriend who made her happy. There was never anything serious between us anyway.'

The cops looked at him as though analysing the inner recesses of his skull but they had to be satisfied with his assurance.

The other boyfriend, the bling guy, was also interviewed and he appeared on TV with Melanie's tearful parents, pleading for her to return.

Only Ludo knew there'd be no coming back, no happy returns.

Two years later, while attending Padminster College where he studied English literature, Ludo came up against a group of wasters who skipped lectures and smoked various illegal substances in the lavatories. Ludo despised such people and had never felt the need for drugs. He got all the kicks he required from exercising his powers. When the leader of this group, a lout called Craig Coglan, offered to sell Ludo a packet of what he called 'the real bigtime stuff', Ludo told him to stick his head up his arse.

Coglan didn't like that. He resembled an older version of Michael O'Connor except that his muscle had already run to flab. He had a tattoo of a mermaid on the back of his right hand: the hand that now grabbed Ludo and shook him like a rat.

'Come here you guys and watch me pulverise this little heap of shit,' Coglan said to his acolytes. And they, sycophantic as ever, gathered around in admiration and expectation of Ludo's humiliation and pain.

Ludo had other ideas. This lot would go into *The Great Beyond*. Accommodating all of them together would of course mean opening the portal wider than he'd ever done before but by now there were no limits to his powers. Inhaling mightily, grinning in a way that incensed Coglan, Ludo said, 'This is where we part company, pal.' And the portal opened wider and wider. Wider than ever before. Too wide.

Suddenly a great clawed tentacle emerged, green and scaly and weeping yellow pus that stank like a charnel house. It wrapped itself around Ludo's neck and yanked him through the portal.

Then immediately, on the other side, he found what it was that had been awaiting all his victims. It was something that even in his most wild imaginings he had never conceived of.

Disappearing, he screamed and screeched. But he didn't hear a thing.

Apparition of Yargatti village
(Shashi Kadapa)

Skeletal hands with the flesh partially stripped away held the handlebars in a tight grip, finger bones with loose flesh stretched tightly. Worn sandals pushed the pedals in jerks, not in the smooth motion of a cyclist. The veins and tendons stood out starkly, pulsating and throbbing with blood squirting out. The arms led to a neck and then... nothing! Utter panic filled his stomach, as he realized that there was no head.

***

I am Bhima, a freelance writer and went to I visited Yargatti village in South India. There was this old man Ajja, grandfather sitting under a banyan tree. People pointed him out when I asked about old folklore. After much pestering, he agreed to tell a story. He asked me to fetch his old leather satchel tied to the cycle. With trembling hands, the old man placed it on his lap and told his story. The story begins during the British rule in India in the early 1900s.

The monster appears

The rain-bearing winds of the monsoon shrieked through the dusk, and the first large rain drops spattered on the new postman, Arvind Deshpande, as he furiously pedaled through a narrow tree-lined path. Bolts of lightning shattered the darkness, filling the evening with bright flashes that showed a long, winding path with bends.

He would soon come to the stone bridge that straddled a small canal through which water flowed to the dam. The water had turned brown with the silt that it carried from the hills. Branches and forest debris floated and bobbed in the current.

Arvind was gasping with the effort as he steadied himself just as the skies opened up, bringing down a deluge. He was midway down the path when he realized that another cyclist was coming up. He was surprised by the Khaki uniform and the satchel. This fellow was from another village?

A bolt of lightning lit up the night as the cyclist came abreast. With a start, Arvind realized that he could only see a black hole where there should have been the man's face.

The light was gone in an instant, and Arvind later recalled the rush of adrenalin that gripped him as he saw the apparition, with skeletal hands gripping the handlebars of the cycle tightly.

Arvind was in a frenzy as he controlled his cycle over the rough cobblestones. The figure seemed to have disappeared in the rain. He muttered to himself, 'bah, darkness and lightning are playing tricks on my mind. Imagine! A rider without a head.'

Arvind rode into his gate, soaking wet, and smiled at his wife, Vani, who was cradling their baby. The gate was made of small wooden frames bolted into two poles that stood in the thick bushes that made up the hedge. Laughing at the chortling baby, he wiped the rain off himself as best as he could and picked up the tot. He loved his family; they were everything to him.

"Vani. You will not believe it. "Something funny happened when I was riding back.

His wife was busy preparing tea and dinner. She looked over her shoulder as Arvind played with the baby.

"What happened?"

I was riding back home and thought I saw another postman cross me on the bridge. I looked at him and saw that he did not have a head.

Then he started laughing at the incident. The baby also joined in, gurgling with his father.

Vani frowned "Without a head? It must be the rain. You did not see him properly? Perhaps there was no rider, and you saw your own shadow. "

The encounter was forgotten as Arvind played with his gurgling baby. He lit another kerosene lamp, and he gossiped with his wife and told her about his colleagues, office politics, local gossip, and petty jealousies and rivalries that are a part of any community.

With the baby asleep, they made love passionately and snuggled, cozy in their warm embrace. Late in the night, Arvind woke to a small hammering sound that seemed to come from outside. "Must be the wind banging the loose gate."

Dawn breaks early in the countryside. Arvind was up and drinking a cup of tea as he gazed out of the window. It had rained heavily the previous night, and water ran everywhere in tiny streams.

Then he saw something brown buried in the ground outside the window. He got up and saw a khaki sack used by postmen to deliver mail. Red liquid was oozing from the sack and making thin trails in the water. Just then, his wife shouted that hot water was ready for his bath. He went in and forgot about the sack. Preoccupied with his pending work at the office, he did not even glance at the area outside his window.

At the post office, he got swept up with work and soon forgot about the cyclist he had met the previous evening. As the other postmen returned to the office in the evening, he remembered the apparition he had met the previous evening. There were four staff members; he and another postman, Basu; Appa, the mail sorter; and Pandhari, who handled money orders.

He casually remarked, "I saw another postman yesterday. In the heavy rain, I could not see him clearly and he appeared to be headless. "

The next instant, there was pin-drop silence!

The staff stared at him with horror, and they shuffled out silently. They stood in the verandah and stood jabbering, looking at Arvind with fear.

Slightly perturbed, Arvind asked, "What is the problem? Why are you muttering among yourselves? You know anything? "

The staff shuffled their feet and looked around furtively, giving no explanation. Arvind shrugged helplessly. He would not get any answer from them. They would talk later, when things had cooled down.

The monster appears again

Distributing salaries to the staff at the post office was one of Arvind's jobs. He picked up the employee register, which had information on salaries paid, leave taken, and other details going back a few decades. When he did not have much to do, Arvind often browsed through the pages and read the notations of his colleagues from long ago.

As he turned the pages, he noticed that one page was torn and only the top half remained. An entry was barely visible. It was the last salary paid to Gopal Rao, employee number 971. Where there should have been a signature, there was only a thumb impression.

This disturbed him. As a rule, only literate postmen were hired. Whose thumb impression could this be?

Scrawled in small, barely legible writing, he made out the words "wife of the deceased." Arvind showed the torn page to Appa and other staff.

"Who tore off this page? This is an offence."

The staff stared fearfully at the torn page and shook their heads.

The mail sorter and the most senior member of staff approached.

"Look at the date. More than 70 years ago, on January 15, 1880."

"How will we find out who ripped the page?"

With a snort of disgust, Arvind put the register down and returned to his work.

With all the mail and money orders delivered and rain threatening to pour down in buckets, he decided to go home early. He bought some groceries and was soon off. His thoughts wandered to his family and his job. He approached the tree-lined path quickly. The branches, heavy with water, had bunched and closed to form a canopy along the path. Diffused light wafted through dimly, covering small patches of darkness.

Arvind suddenly realized that he had company. He looked back to see another cyclist coming up fast behind him.

The cyclist was now just a few paces behind him, and he could hear his furious pedaling. He sneaked a look behind as he slowed down to let the other fellow catch up. From the corner of his eye, he saw a bicycle wheel come into his view; the handlebars were dimly glinting in the dark. A pair of khaki-clad pants pedaled hard. Arvind jerked his eyes at the dark road ahead as he stumbled into a pothole, regained balance, and then glanced sideways again.

Skeletal hands with the flesh partially stripped away held the handlebars in a tight grip, finger bones with loose flesh stretched tightly. Worn sandals pushed the pedals in jerks, not in the smooth motion of a cyclist. The veins and tendons stood out starkly, pulsating and throbbing with blood squirting out. The arms led to a neck and then... nothing! Utter panic filled his stomach, as he realized that there was no head.

The monster raised its hand to try to catch him. Arvind's first reaction was to get down and accost the rider. This unexpected sight unnerved him and he bolted. Rising from the seat, he shifted his weight to the handles and started pushing the pedals with all he had.

Arvind took the first bend at full speed, skidding on the gravel. The rider followed close behind, and Arvind could hear a harsh, rasping sound. Then he was down the straight, pushing away and nearing the second bend. As he went into the turn, the rider shot into the inside lane, and Arvind had to apply the brakes abruptly to avoid crashing into him.

Arvind was getting irritated at the tricks this fellow was playing. He reached out to catch the fellow. His cycle went into a runt, and his hands moved back to hold the handles and correct his balance.

Swerving away sharply, Arvind saw the hand waving, as if asking him to stop. The fingers were torn and the skin clung loosely to the finger bones. This was getting scary. His house was nearby, and he did not want this thing to accompany him to his house.

Fighting down his disgust and with sweat pouring down his back, he pumped the pedals into a blur. Light beckoned from the edge of the canopy of branches. He felt that if he could reach the light with the apparition, he could see clearly and catch the scoundrel.

The rider led him closely. His satchel cover had come loose and flopped over. The contents jerked and bounced with the motion. The next instant, Arvind was on the next bend and took it sharply, going into a tight curve with the bicycle tilting dangerously.

Arvind went faster, pumping the pedals with all he had. His front wheel was almost touching the apparition's pedals. The satchel cover of the apparition came untied and its contents glistened in the lightning. Arvind glanced down and almost fell off as he saw the contents.

A severed neck, bumped in the sack. It was the most horrendous sight he had seen. Lightning flashed, and in the brief flash, he saw blood congealed from severed arteries and the nerves, stringy and wet, hung limp and lifeless. Bloodied eyeballs rolled loose in the sockets. Skin peeled from the skull, and the mouth grimaced in a tortured cry.

He flashed through the light and was in the open. He saw a bullock cart come up the road. He braked hard, skidded and fell. Comforting hands picked him up and carried him to the cart. In a haze from the fall, he gazed back at the path instinctively. The rider has vanished.

He lay in the cart, frustrated and angry, mumbling incoherently about a headless cyclist. The passengers, mainly laborers who worked at the nearby dam, carried him into his house.

Arvind's wife huddled around her husband, not knowing what to do. Her tense face was streaked with tears. Arvind slipped into a fitful sleep.

The door slowly creaked open, and the headless cyclist stood in the doorway. Rain dripped from his clothes and gathered in puddles around his legs. He held the severed head in his hands and Arvind watched, unable to move. His wide-open eyes watched the figure advance into the room,

81

beckoning him. The head opened its mouth and spoke in a harsh, rasping voice, "Come, it is time."

Arvind screamed loudly as he felt icy cold hands on his neck and awoke with a jerk. His wife was shaking him, asking if he was all right. He wildly looked around the room, shivering in his sweat-drenched clothes. The door was firmly closed, the latch drawn; there was no one there. It was a nightmare. He went into a deep, dreamless sleep as his wife patted his head soothingly.

He awoke in the morning with his limbs contorted in pain from the fall and stress of the previous night. He had a slight fever and a runny nose. He stretched to ease some of the stiffness as his wife walked in.

"What happened? Did something frighten you? You kept mumbling in your sleep about a headless figure. You even screamed a couple of times. Don't you remember? "

Arvind felt the words almost spilling out of him, but his ego and care for his wife forced him to keep quiet. There was no point in frightening her. He stood up stiffly and beckoned a villager passing by his house. He sent a message to the post office through him saying that he was sick and would not be coming in for the day.

The monster's tale

Word of Arvind's exploits the previous evening got around fast in the small community, and the local gossip monger, the crone Gangawwa, turned up. Her main pastime was to visit homes, gather information, add her bit to it, and then spread it around.

She was bent over, walked with a stick, and it was reputed that she was a witch. She earned her income by casting black magic spells or by removing them. No one really believed that her magic was effective. However, just to keep themselves on the right side of all spirits and not antagonize anybody, they visited her hut every Saturday and bought the customary lemon and chilies charm to ward off bad luck, a lemon strung with chilies.

After accepting a cup of tea from Vani, Gangawwa blurted out, "Did the sahib really see the headless cyclist?"

Arvind still felt high-spirited and unsteady in spite of a mostly restful day. He sat up in his armchair, resentful that people refused to accept his story at face value.

"You old woman, you dare to doubt me. Anyway, what do you know about this apparition? Tell me about this ghost or whatever. What is it, why does it seek me out?'"

Gangawwa settled comfortably on the floor and asked for another cup of tea.

"Is the sahib aware that the house he lives in is built on an old shamshan, or graveyard?"

Seeing the stricken looks on their faces, Gangavva expanded on it with relish.

"Many years ago, this area was a small private graveyard of the big landlord, The Desai. There was no road back then and there was jungle everywhere.

The Desais' were cruel and villagers reported seeing many demons and evil spirits in this area."

She continued, pausing to sip tea.

"This happened a long time ago. I was only a child then. The government acquired the land to build the dam. Surplus land was used to build government quarters. The dam swallowed the landlord's house and the surrounding orchards. The graveyard, which sat on a hillock, was spared from being submerged. I remember the post office had just come up and people could exchange letters. All you needed was someone to read and write the postcards. There was a postman called Gopal Rao who had died horribly."

Arvind through rapdilu 'Gopal? Gopal! The name is in the register, on the torn page. The half-legible name What could possibly be the connection here?'

He had a vivid flashback of hurtling through the night on his bicycle with the headless cyclist in hot pursuit. He sat up, retching and coughing from the stress and the cold. Vani rushed to him to pat his forehead. Gangavva was admonished and driven out.

He went back to sleep, and the morning slipped away in a daze. Late in the afternoon, Appa dropped in. He gazed intently at Arvind, seeing lines of stress on the tense face.

Arvind burst out in anger, "Who was this, Gopal? Why did he die? Was this headless cyclist real?"

Raising his hands, Appa began, "Gopal Rao was one of the first postmen in this area. This was many decades ago.

He continued, "The Desai, landlord or dhanyaru, was cruel and usurped the land of poor farmers. He liked music and organized meets where singers and musicians were invited to perform and were handsomely paid. Once, Gopal Rao had to deliver a letter to Desai. Since the landlord was illiterate, he asked Gopal to read the letter to him. It was from the district magistrate and was an order to the landlord to surrender his land for the dam. The Desai was a man of a fiery temper and was a scion of the local king. Surrendering his land was like paying tribute to a conqueror, an insult, and this was unacceptable.

Appa paused to wipe his face, then resumed.

In a fit of rage, he pulled out his sword and beheaded the postman. He then buried the headless body in the family graveyard. The head was thrown away so that the victim could never attain moksha. "

"What has this got to do with me?" Anger and outrage flooded Arvind's voice.

Appa continued, "The postman became a monster and roams the countryside, searching for its head. The landlord and his family drowned in the waters of the dam. "

Appa continued his story, "It is said that the monster will rest in peace only if a male heir of the landlord offers the head back to the spirit. However, this is not possible since, as far as we know, the family died out. There are rumors that one son was spirited away by a loyal servant. However, the son and his heirs have not appeared until now. Therefore, the headless postman roams this land forever, killing whom he likes. "

Angrily, Arvind burst out, "I do not believe this one bit. But why me? Why is this thing haunting me? "

Calmly, Appa replied, "Rumor says it that the headless demon marks a person at random and takes the victim's head in the belief that it is its head. The apparition manifests once in a while, and a horrible death has always befallen someone."

Quick to love deeply and even quicker to get angry, Arvind exploded. "But why come after me? Will it harm my family? I swear to God I will kill it if it even comes near my wife and kid. "

Appa smiled, "Saheb, the monster is already dead. You cannot kill it. As far as coming after you, I don't know. Perhaps it wants your head. "

***

Vani was very worried about her husband. Yes, someone's evil eye has fallen on him. She approached Gangawwa and asked for a lucky charm amulet to be made for him. The crone was still nursing some anger for being driven off the last time she saw Arvind. Vani enticed her with money and fruits. Somewhat mollified, Gangawwa hammered out an amulet from a small brass sheet, inscribed it with symbols to ward off Shani, the god who was best worshipped to keep off bad luck. Then she made a great show of spitting on the ground around the amulet to ward off bad luck, tied it on a string and asked Vani to make her husband wear it around the neck.

She also strung up lemons and chilies along with a small black doll to make two garlands of the stuff and asked Vani to hang them in front of the main and rear doors of their home.

Vani said, "He drives a bicycle. What about that? "

"Oh, yes. Warding off the evil eye for the cycle is very important. "

She proceeded to make another garland and asked Vani to tie it on the front of the cycle.

Then she added, "Take your husband to the Panchalingeshwara temple, the holy temple of Shiva. "Only Shiva can remove the curse that has struck him."

Arvind stoutly refused to bow to these superstitious beliefs. He said he would look foolish and face ridicule if he went around on his cycle with a lucky charm made of lemon and chilies. To mollify and keep his wife happy, Arvind wore it around his neck, complaining that it scratched his chest.

Visit the Panchalingeshwara temple

Appa and Vani prevailed on Arvind to obtain the divine blessings of Shiva at the Panchalingeshwara temple. Built in the 11th century by the Badami Chalukya kings, the inner sanctum, or the Garbhagruha, had three shivalingas in a straight line and two on either side. Arvind stood with his features distorted and suffused. Clearly, his mind was battling a complex issue.

Appa asked him, "What is the matter?"

"I don't know. I can remember seeing this complex, the carvings, the statues, and the lingams. I get the feeling I have seen these things earlier, even come here before. "

Arvind turned to look into the corner and noticed something standing there. It was the headless apparition, pointing at the structure. What! This thing is following me around when I am with my family!

Rage overcame him and he rushed at the apparition to catch it. He stumbled over a step and fell. The injury was minor, but his anger and outrage at the specter of following his family inflamed him. Appa and other people carried him and sat him under a tree.

Vani stood forlornly clutching the baby, 'What is wrong with my husband?'

The old acharya of the temple came over. Appa knew him, and they went to a corner away from the two.

"Guruji, our postmaster, Arvind, has been behaving very strangely for the past few days. He says that he saw the headless postman. What is the problem? "

The acharya said, "I fear Arvind is possessed by an evil spirit that will gain control of his mind and then Arvind will die."

"What can we do?"

The evil spirit has to be exorcised and driven away. We have to go to Saundatti, where Devi Yellamma resides. I know the chief, Magti Vaidya, the main tantric priest. We will see if that can be done.

When the plans were announced, Arvind became belligerent and obstinately refused to get exorcised. His ego prevented him from accepting that he was possessed.

He asked, "How will it look the next time I deliver the mail? People will ask me about the evil spirit. Everyone respects me here and I will look foolish. "

Vani cried, threw tantrums, beat her breasts, tore her hair and finally he agreed. He was extremely skeptical of such practices, but he loved his wife and was ready to take this step for her.

The Exorcism

One afternoon, Appa, Guruji, Arvind, and Vani went one hour to Saundatti and the temple of goddess Yellamma. Built in the 3rd century CE, the temple on the Saundatti Betta has seen many additions and improvements. The temple is dedicated to the goddess Yellamma, or Renuka, the goddess of fertility and Saptamatrika, the seven divine mothers. It was believed that anyone who worshipped at the temple would see their problems disappear.

The Magti Vaidya welcomed them and then looked at Arvind. He gave him a concoction of milk and bhang mixed with sugar. The drink had a soporific effect and rendered docile belligerent hosts such as Arvind and their infestations docile and docile.

The arena for the tantra was beaten hard to make it firm and then smeared with cow dung. Rice powder and chalk were used to draw rangoli patterns and rectangular spaces on the floor. These spaces were drawn in concentric circles around the center, where a fire was burning.

The squares represented a set of demons, and while there were more than 87,000 daityas, or demons, in Hindu mythology, only a few spaces were made to represent leaders. The subject of the ritual was seated in a circle. Flowers, bananas, and neem leaves were liberally spread across the arena along with clay pots, whisk brooms, and some hens, which sat in enclosures at the back. A hen would be sacrificed only if the ritual or a demon demanded it.

There was another darker aspect that was not openly acknowledged. This was the human sacrifice for tantric magic, a very powerful magic used for only the most severe infestations. They did not consider the human sacrifice ritual.

Arvind was helped to his feet, the effects of Bhang still strong. He was in a trance but supported like a drunk by Appa and Guruji. He was seated in the circle facing east, and flowers were arranged along the circumference. The drum beaters, or dholak players, and flute players, their faces and torsos smeared with ash, were seated outside the circle. A small fire was started.

The master, Magti Vaidya, shouted, "Yajamana (gentleman), you are placed in the circle and as I start asking questions, you have to answer. The drums will beat continually, rattling and confusing the demon inside you. It will want to come out, but it cannot escape the circle and we can trap it.

The master started his intonation of mantras and formulaic invocations to the great gods and to Devi Yelamma. Then he started chanting the mantras with full force, while looking at Arvind closely. He wanted the daitya's name so that the appropriate spell could be used. He blew hard at the smoke and brandished a broom. The rituals begin.

Arvind slowly swayed to the beats of the drums and the sound of the flute, moving slowly where he sat. The master shouted, "Come on, tell me your name."

"Arvindn Raghvendra Kulkarni."

"What is your caste and gotra?"

"Brahmin, Vasistha gotra."

"Where were you born?"

"Dharwad."

"What is your father's and grandfather's name?"

"My father's name is Vitthal Kulkarani, and my grandfather's name is Narayan Kulkarni."

"What is your great-grandfather's name?"

Arvind started trembling and shaking. He tried to get up from the circle, but the master's assistants forced him down.

The master repeated the question, "What is your great-grandfather's name?"

The master repeated the question a few more times, and it only served to drive Arvind mad. No answer was forthcoming. He thrashed about and would have run away but for the three stout, strong, and large assistants who struggled to hold him.

The master noted the answers with a frown. When the question about his great-grandfather was asked, his rage and fear gave him this strength, and he wanted to break free.

The master moved back, wanting to allow Arvind to calm down. In this present state, any further questions would cause a nervous breakdown.

He signaled the musicians to continue their songs. He asked them to play a repertoire of old folk songs that were popular about 70 years ago. The intention was to have the old spirit, if any, in Arvind's body manifest itself when the favorite music was played. It was also possible that the spirit would try to harm Arvind in anger for being woken up.

The musicians moved between different ballads and songs by Bhagwan Basavanna, several vacahanas, and then one of them started playing a racy ballad, Periyapattanada Kalaga. This song narrated the battle and tales of bravery between the King of Mysore and the King of Periyapattana.

Arvind stopped thrashing as the song started. Then he began to sing in an old Kannada dialect used by the upper castes some decades back. The master noted this.

The drums started with a crescendo and then settled to a steady beat as the Master came close to Arvind.

"Why have you entered this body?"

"I have not entered this body."

"What do you want from Arvind? He will do what you want if you promise to leave his body. "

"I have not entered this body."

Who are you?"

"Someone ancient that Arvind knows."

"Why have you entered this body?"

"I was in his blood from the beginning."

And so it went for quite some time. Nothing was happening. Matagati Vaidya eventually stopped the rituals since there was nothing to exorcise.

The master offered another drink to Arvind to counter the sedative. His assistants carried Arvind to a hut beyond, and Vani sat with him, sick with worry. Arvind laid his head on her lap and slept.

***

The master motioned Appa and Guruji aside.

"He is not possessed by any external spirit."

"What! Then what about the answers to your questions and dancing to the music? "

"I think it is a family curse. It appears that an ancestor, probably his great grandfather or another past forefather, has not been appeased. Maybe they did a bad deed, killed someone and did not let the soul of the reclaimed person be liberated. Do you know anything about his great grandfather? Yajamana goes violent when he is mentioned."

Appa replied, "We do not know. Our employee records only ask for the father's name and place of birth. "

The master said, "As I said, it is possible that the great-grandfather did something evil. His progeny wanted to remove all association with the person, fearing that the stigma would haunt them. Over the generations, no trace of the person remains in the memory."

Guruji asked, "Master, what about the headless apparition that haunts him?"

"There was no sign of the apparition. It does not inhibit his body, else it would have identified itself. Yajamana must have heard or read stories of this ghost and decided to use its manifestation. "

Appa asked, "What do we do now?"

"There is nothing we can do now. Let things remain as they are. Always keep someone with him when he goes out to deliver letters and when he returns home. I feel that he will get over this spirit. "

Recovering the satchel

The exorcism had not cast out any evil spirits. However, Arvind was now nervous and angry. He huddled in his house, angry and resentful at the manner in which people looked at him.

He yearned for one more encounter with the specter. He was prepared to send it to hell and back. What did it think? That he would become a gibbering victim of its terror tactics?

Sleep was far from Arvind's mind. Then he remembered the buried piece of sacking that he had seen from the window a few days back. The sack started eating into his mind, drawing him in, urging and goading him to get up and dig it up that very night.

Eager to investigate, he took a pickaxe and the lamp and went out. The rain had stopped, and the moon shone through tendrils of clouds. The piece of sacking lay immersed in a small pool of water.

Arvind tugged at the sacking, and it started to come free in the wet soil. It seemed to be snagged by something underneath, and he wanted to dig it free. An owl swooped through the night sky and brushed his head.

The bushes that made up the hedge of his cottage rustled with the wind. The branches, heavy with rainwater, dipped and swung, showering him with each passing gust.

The first few hits with the pickaxe loosened the earth. He tugged at the sack. Nothing happened. Something was holding it in place. Putting aside the pickaxe, he caught hold of the sack and pulled with both hands. The sacking tore loose, with the bottom still buried in the ground. Something dull glittered in the moonlight, and he bent down, tugging at the piece still stuck in the ground.

The sack came loose, still held by something under the ground. Then Arvind saw the number on the sack: "971". The ripped page in the registry - Gopal Rao - his beheading - his hasty burial...Was this spot where the wretched soul lay buried?

Eager to explore, he dug further and found that the sack was snagged on a rectangular piece of wood with a sign carved on the face. He dug with his fingers and brought out the wooden piece.

It had carvings and the names of gods in Sanskrit. Figures of gods were carved on the faces. He had seen these motifs recently. Where?.. Yes, it was at the temple. These carvings were from the temple. But how did the carvings appear on this piece and what was it doing here? He had no answers.

The moon went behind the clouds and it started raining again. The hedge bushes parted, a shadow fell on him, and he found himself looking up into the maws of the headless demon. The rain fell directly into the hollow of the collar, where the head should have been, and bloodied water spurted forth in small droplets.

The apparition lifted its arms, beckoning him to follow, urging him to come forward. Arvind wanted to grab and shake it, but felt strangely powerless and weak-willed. The clouds were gone and the full moon shone brightly lighting up the countryside in a soft light.

In a trance, he followed the specter, unwilling yet unresisting, as it turned and glided through the forest. Then it finally stopped at the very edge of the cliff overlooking a lake created by the dam's backwaters. The apparition seemed to point to something in the yonder. Arvind could make out a land mass in the distance.

The apparition dove into the water and started swimming towards the island, looking back to urge him to follow. The evening's exertion and stress took their toll, and Arvind collapsed on the precipice in a swoon, clutching the sack and wooden board in his hand.

When he jerked awake, the sun had risen beyond the treetops. A search party, led by Appa and Vani, found him on the cliff, and they carried him back. He lay on the bed, with the wood piece and the sack on the floor.

***

The night's events were vivid in his mind. It seemed that the spirit did not wish to kill him. It could have easily done so if it wished. Instead, it

96

wanted Arvind to go to the island. Why and why him? He would not rest until he found the answer.

Arvind examined the piece of wood carefully and realized that it had once been part of a motif on a door. A series of flower patterns and symbols of gods were engraved along the length. The figure of Yellamma, the local goddess, was engraved in the middle. The corner had broken off.

Two small holes on the sides of the panel with streaks of rust showed that nails had been used to fasten the piece to the door. Small scratch marks ran across the face of the piece. They could have been caused by a small animal, or by raking fingernails as someone struggled in their death throes. He was driven by an urgent need to know the details of the panel. Who better to ask than the village carpenter?

He reached the post office to meet the silent, questioning eyes of his colleagues. No one wanted to ask him directly, but everyone wanted to know about his wanderings. Curious villagers turned up and found some pretext to look at and talk with him, and after seeing him, they sadly shook their heads and told each other that the fellow was already dead.

The morning passed in a whirl of activity. By afternoon, his work was over, and he set out to meet the village carpenter. He saw him sitting in front of his hut, sawing away at a plank. On seeing Arvind, he got up, folded his hands in greeting, and asked him to come inside.

After exchanging pleasantries, Arvind showed the piece of wood to the carpenter, asking him where it came from. It had a fine scent, and the carpenter looked closely at it.

"Sandalwood. This must be a part of the panel of a pooja room. The design is rather old-fashioned. I have never seen such a pattern other than in old manors. Where did Saheb find this?'

Not wanting to give the details to the carpenter, Arvind made up some story about finding it washed up in the stream.

The carpenter raised his arms helplessly, hoping that perhaps his grandfather would know.

"Is he here? Can we ask him? "

The grandfather was very old and was sleeping in a corner, just holding on to life.

Softly nudging him awake and saying that the old man was deaf, the carpenter asked him.

"Ajja, the postmaster sahib has come to meet you. Please look here. "

He showed the wooden piece to Ajja. The old man squinted, brought it close to his eyes, felt it across with his gnarled fingers and started to cry. His replies were incoherent and Arvind had to strain to catch what was said.

"Alas, Hire (elder) Dhanyaru, such a fine family, so kind-hearted. Then the eldest son took over the estate and everything started going down. "

The old man lapsed into meaningless jabber, then became coherent.

"Yes, he had prepared the pooja room. Dhanyaru wanted it to look like the Panchalingeshwara temple... very nicely decorated... fancy carvings... all made of sandalwood and teak... He had this headpiece carved... It was placed on top of the idol of Lord Shiva.. such an inauspicious event.. the cut off head.. 'Blood spilled...

The old man dozed off to sleep, tears rolling from his eyes. The carpenter led Arvind out; nothing more could be known.

***

Arvind wanted to know the location of the old house where Desai, the landlord, once lived and where the postmen had allegedly been beheaded.

The Registrar at the land office said, "Dam waters now flow over the vast acres that the landlord owned. The whole area is under water. Any secret the place holds is lost forever. "

This was not true. He had seen the temple the other night.

" I went the other night to the top of the precipice that looks over the dam backwaters. I did see the island and the temple. It is there. "

The Registrar replied, "Post Master Sahib, that is not possible. The estate of the landlord is the deepest water. There was a small hillock on which the house and temple once stood, but the dam swallowed it up. "

Confused, Arvind wondered about the island and the trees he had seen. Had he imagined them? Was he imagining the apparition? No one had seen it except him. Well, maybe...

Arvind and Appa left and walked to the tree-lined path that stood in front of him, and he dreaded going through it again. There was a longer, circuitous track over a hill that bypassed the path, and they decided to take it.

Small bushes and rocks littered the track as they climbed the hill. A small temple with an idol of the village deity, goddess Yellamma, stood at the top. Arvind stopped to rest and, after bowing to the Devi, turned to look at the magnificent scenery down below.

The dam's backwaters flowed below, touching the foothills. He could see the dam sluice gates from afar. The valley through which the river flowed had lush green forests, swaying in the wind. To the left, he could see his village and could guess the approximate position of his house. To the right were green forests that extended to meet the horizon, covered in an intermittent mist.

With a start, he realized that the landlord's farms and house would have been on the slope on the far right. Through the rolling mists, he could make out a hillock that formed an island and a small structure in the distance. Part of a wall was dimly visible. The wall, broken in places, ran south and ended in a canopy that would have been the main house.

They came home. The next two days were holidays, and he decided to explore the structure he had seen from the hilltop. Appa had dropped by.

He casually mentioned, "Look Sahib, you can apply for an immediate transfer to another faraway location."

"Transfer? Why? What will people think of me? That I am a coward and ran away when I could not handle something. "

"I was only thinking of you and your family."

"Never mind my health Appa. I will be fine once this thing is over. Did those hills, that island, and the broken walls, did they belong to the landlord? "

"What hillock, what island, what wall? There is only water. "

"I'm talking about the island we saw from the hill."

"Sahib, you are again imagining things. There is nothing there but water. How could you have seen it?"

Laughing in frustration and anger, Arvind went inside. Everyone was lying; they were being over-protective. He knew what he saw. He had seen the house and its outer walls. Well, there was only one way to find out – he had no choice but to go there. He had to solve the mystery for his sanity and the safety of his wife and baby.

Visit the Island

Early the next morning, before his wife woke up, he went down to the lake shore, met a fisherman, and asked him to take him across.

The fisherman was not willing to do this. "No Saheb! The other side is taboo. There are whirlpools, and anyone who went there never came back."

Arvind offered him five rupees. He would hire the boat for a day. After many threats and counterarguments, the fisherman finally relented and handed over the boat. Arvind tried out the boat and kept his sack with the broken wooden panel and the torn sacking he had dug up.

"Turn back by afternoon, Sahib, as the current starts flowing to the far side. You will remain stranded on the far shore if you delay. Watch out for rocks and whirlpools. There is a water skin with fresh water, some food, a kerosene lamp, some bandages, matches, and an axe if you need them."

***

While Arvind was not an expert at handling boats, he had ridden in them often and could manage the vessel. He set off, rowing with slow, leisurely strokes in the direction where he had seen the structure. He had plotted an approximate course that would take him to the required location.

The small waves had turned choppy and the undertow was deciding its course. Arvind hunched forward and started rowing forcefully. The normally placid waters seemed to have strong undercurrents, and they pulled him across to the far side.

After half an hour of rowing, a small rock loomed in the early morning mist. It rose from the lake depths and stood like a sentinel guarding the temple. He pulled around it and then an undercurrent caught him. The current carried him steadily forward with force, and all he had to do was to slip an oar on each side and paddle in the right direction.

The hill and the ruined walls appeared as faint silhouettes. They became sharper as the boat approached the structure. Arvind gauged the distance to the edifice and paddled to the right. The current was taking him where he wanted to go.

He saw a piece of driftwood floating along, and then suddenly it whipped forward, going incredibly fast. He watched with rapt attention as it bounced among the waves, then circled very fast before it disappeared into the water.

Whirlpool!

With wide eyes, he saw the whirlpool just ahead and to his left. The rim of the whirlpool went round in crazy circles, now rising and then falling, white froth dripping from the edges. It hissed and bubbled like a serpent as it went around, moving with the current, sucking whatever came its way.

Arvind pulled at the oars in the opposite direction with all he had, trying to get away. The outer edge of the cone of the whirlpool was just a few oar lengths from his boat, and Arvind got a close look at the terrifying sight inside.

The cone went around in a hypnotic swirl. The walls seemed incredibly smooth and edged with white foam that broke every now and then to send up a fine spray. The mouth opened and closed, giving out large bubbles. Arvind fought hard, feeling the boat slip into the funnel. One end hung in the air, and as the boat spun fast, he felt his head going giddy.

The next instant, he was out of the grip as the whirlpool threw his boat away. The hillock was nearby, and he limply pulled the boat ashore. Then he sank to the ground, trembling and weak with exhaustion.

***

Arvind staggered up and marked his bearings. The structure he had seen would be to his right. The

103

path was thick with bushes, and water ran through the underbrush. He drew out the axe he had taken from the boat, and hacked his way through the dense underbrush and entered a small clearing.

He could make out a masonry structure under patches of slippery green moss. It's odd that the jungle has spread everywhere, but this small patch has no trees or bushes. Was this place so evil that even the jungle refused to claim it?

The moss clung to the walls, dripping and wet. He scraped it and saw the huge outer wall underneath. It had been built a long time ago as a mini fortress, and the wall was about five feet thick. As per ancient vastushastra, the main door would be facing north-east and the pooja room would be on the same side.

Stepping carefully, he made his way across the wall and then saw a raised portion where the wall met the main doorway. A narrow passage ran along the inner length, and Arvind guessed this must be where the soldiers stood on guard.

He approached the raised portion and peered over the side to see a large doorframe. Climbing down carefully, he stood in front of the huge stone doorway. The wooden doors had rotted long ago, and only rusting hinges remained.

Then he saw the goddess Yellamma's image, carved on the wooden frame that still remained with a part broken off. From his satchel, he pulled out the wooden piece that he had dug out of his garden and fitted it on the door. It was a perfect fit.

The wind had started blowing with full force, and in the distance, he could hear jackals howling. The wind seemed to be whispering come on in.

Arvind he realized he had company. He turned back quickly, thinking he saw something streak into the bushes. The jungle sounds had almost stopped, and he could hear his own breath coming in harsh rasps.

He stepped through the doorway carefully and was inside. The roof had fallen in many places, and he could make out piles of rubble everywhere.

He made his way to the courtyard where the cows would have been tethered. Just beyond was the raised platform, running along the length of the house and which would lead to the rooms where people lived. To the left, he could see a small platform on which the landlord probably reclined and governed.

A small noise behind made him turn.

There! Something streaked again across the background.

He shouted, "Who is there? Come out and show yourself. I know you are there. "

His voice resounded through the structure. Nothing moved, and he could hear his voice echoing through the ruins.

He saw a couple of steps to the right, and these led to a room with a low ceiling and a deep pit. This would be the granary, where food grains were stored. He turned back the way he had come and saw another small passage.

The passage led to a small room, and Arvind realized that he was in front of the sanctum of the pooja room. A stone statue of the village deity stood guard at the entrance. Arranged in the room were the five Shiva lingams he had seen in the temple back in the village.

A rusted hook swung above from the ceiling, and this was where the temple bell would have hung. Normally, visitors rang the bell before entering the sanctum and prayed at the Shiva Lingams. This bell was long gone, and the chain holding the bell to the hook was rusted.

The landlord had been a devotee of Shiva, and he had taken care to replicate the interior of the Panchalingeshwara temple and the Garbhagruhas in his home. While the ancient temple had figures carved in granite, the skills needed for granite sculpture were not available locally. Besides, granite carvings would take decades to complete. Hence, he had asked carpenters to carve out the motifs in sandalwood.

The walls and the ceiling were still covered with sandalwood. Long immersion in water had made the wood moist and soft, and some pieces had fallen off, while others hung limply.

A cold apprehension filled him as he approached the room. Was this the end of his troubles? Was this the place where he would find answers to his torment?

***

He slowly stepped inside the lowered doorway and stood in the sanctum sanctorum. It was dark and he had to peer to see what was inside. Some parts of the inner walls were covered with marble, the slabs broken and dirt spilling out, while the other areas had sandalwood. In the corner was a pedestal where the Shiva idol would have been placed. At the base of the pedestal were small furrows to allow the water used in the pooja to run off to a small cistern and to the garden beyond. The five Shiva lingams were arranged so that water from the idol would wash the lingams.

Small furrows were carved in the granite pedestal. The furrows were encrusted with grime and dirt. They had carried the holy water for a long time, and now stood neglected and broken. The walls had small niches for oil lamps. Patches of dark oil were still visible. In the corner, just behind the pedestal, was a small mound.

Something moved on the floor, glistening and wet. Something was flowing from the mound and running through the furrows, drenching his foot. He looked down uncomprehending. Then the realization flooded him. It was blood, oozing out of the walls and lamps, and running in small threads along the floor.

He turned back in panic, and froze. His heart almost stopped and then speeded up like never before. The apparition stood at the door. The headless apparition had finally come seeking him. It stood silently; a bleeding head held in its hands. It spoke to his mind telepathically, and he could understand what it was saying.

"Dhanyaru."

As it came nearer, images flashed in his head. With deep loathing, he realized this was his family's horrid past.

He was Arvind Desai Dhanyaru, the heir and descendent of the evil landlord,.

His brain was numb with the onslaught of images from the past.

The landlord was performing pooja. Just then, the postman entered, eager to receive some baksheesh when he delivered the letter and read it out. The postman started reading. At first with confidence, then with a trembling voice as he read out the notice written by the district collector to confiscate the lands...

"Respected Desai, landlord. The government is constructing a dam in the area. To complete the construction, we are acquiring your land. Suitable compensation will be given to you as per the rules. We request you to vacate the premises with immediate effect."

The landlord got up then... cursing the collector... cursing the postman... He grabbed a sword and swung at the postman, slashing his chest... The postman stumbled back... went crashing down against the idol and tried weakly to scramble out the door... As he visibly weakened in sheer desperation, he clung to the sandalwood carving at the door, breaking a fragment as he collapsed... The landlord swung his sword again and cut off the postman's head. The he threw the sword in a corner.

-- *the head... the head... that was what it wanted.*

Arvind desperately tried to recall, '*Were did the landlord bury the head? If the head was not found, his head would be chopped off.*'

There under the mound.

108

Arvind dug the dirt frantically, his fingers bleeding from the rough soil and gravel, but continued, nevertheless.

The apparition now hovered behind his back; the skeletal hands had picked up the sword as it prepared to cut off Arvind's head.

Just then, Arvind's fingers touched something smooth. He brushed the soil off it, and it seemed to glisten in the light. He hurriedly pulled out the skull and offered it to the apparition.

The sword clattered to the ground as the apparition bowed before Arvind Desai Dhanyaru, the great grandson of the landlord.

A deep sigh seemed to emanate from the walls as the ghost accepted the skull and fitted it back onto its neck. Then it retreated, going through the walls and disappeared. That is all it ever wanted. This saga has now ended.

A deep rumble startled Arvind. The walls started to crumble, and the floor began to tremble.

Water began to seep in from the walls, and soon it would inundate the structure. He rushed out and stumbled through the creepers. At the shore, he saw the boat bobbing as waves lapped.

He jumped into the boat and started rowing. There was a huge thunderclap and a rush of air, which propelled his boat forward. He looked back and saw the island disappear under the waters of the dam. A dust cloud appeared over the waters and slowly started following Arvind.

Arvind knew that he had to go fast. He pulled out and rowed like a man possessed, trying to escape from the island and his past. He was just a hundred meters away from the now sunk island when the whirlpool appeared.

It glided across the waters in a whorl of hissing, gurgling, bubbles and rushed to intercept the boat. The wind and waves changed directions, pushing the boat forward towards the whirl of death.

It was clear that the island wanted to take the descendant of the landlord. There was no escaping the hiss of water as it gripped his boat and started spinning it around the periphery and pulling the boat into the funnel.

Slowly at first, then rapidly, Arvind felt the pressure of the spin almost tearing his body apart. As he sank into the funnel, he looked up. The apparition watched him, the skull in its place and the skeleton full.

As he started sinking deeper into the funnel, the last image in Arvind's mind was of Vani and the baby.

***

The old man came out of his trance and whispered, "Search parties went around the shore searching for Arvind. The fisherman had told the search parties that he had lent Arvind a boat and that the postmaster had been speaking of an island far beyond before he left with the boat. They found the battered boat, but there was no sign of Arvind. Soon after, Vani and the baby left the village shortly, and no one knew what happened to them. After Arvind's disappearance, the demon never reappeared."

***

The old man dozed off to sleep, tired after his story.

I thanked the old man for the story. Fascinating story. Maybe I could use it. It would be a good piece in a horror anthology collection.

As I got up to leave, I glanced at the satchel on the bench. *The hair on my scalp stiffened; my flesh crawled with goose pimples. The satchel's brass plate twinkled as I stared at the number on it—971.*

Call of the Kindling, Wane of the Moon. (SJ Townend)

He was desperate to know where nearly-babies came from and she said she knew. The girl with the long, tangled plaits and the chipped front tooth said she knew where the babies came from, and the boy figured the girl, his neighbour, had been right about other things so far, like how the sun would never come out again, so he had no reason not to believe her.

Since before the start of dark summer, the wood-skinned babes had appeared in glowing crops around the countryside in which the boy lived. These kindling depositions, these bundles of half-alive joy had been all the boy had thought about: something to hold, something to cherish. An obsession.

The cobbled streets usually a-throng with busy villagers had been empty for days, the bakers and the greengrocers were closed, all of their shelves bare. Mr Nevis, the postman with the oiled ginger curls who whistled a songless tune, had stopped delivering post a month back and he had been the last adult the boy had spoken to.

"Everyone has a nearly-baby. The whole village has disappeared, must've got their babes and nested up. Must've done," the boy said to the girl.

"Everyone, it appears, except for us," the snaggle-toothed girl replied. "Is it because we aren't good enough?"

"I have no idea," he said.

"Come," the girl said. "Let's get moving." She shone her torch on the cart by her feet. "If we find a birthing spot, we can pull back more babes back in this."

"Makes sense," said the boy.

"I'm sure the map will take us straight to the source."

He wondered what she'd look like, as a mother, this girl he'd known for all eleven years of his life, his neighbour. At only a year and a month older than him, he wasn't sure she'd be any good at it and he certainly felt he wasn't ready for parenthood, but didn't feel he had a choice. "We've got to find them," he said. "They'd be orphaned without us. No one would find them as everyone in the village is already busy with theirs. No one else is free to activate them."

To be an orphan meant no parents, no one to tuck you in at night and kiss you on the forehead and slice up an apple into neat segments. The boy had found cutting up and preparing his own food a challenge. The sharp knife his mother had never let him use before had hurt him when his fingers had slipped the night before. Orphaned was exactly how he'd felt since his mother had become preoccupied with her nearly baby. The boy sighed. The warmth of his exhalation hung in the otherwise silent black air between the two children for a short moment. He wanted to ask her if she felt the same, unloved, unlovable, but he decided to change the subject. She could change her mind about all of it, their desperate quest, if he became emotional. "Do you

113

think they're airlifted in from somewhere? And if so, by who?" he said. "And why?"

"Does it really matter how they get here?" The girls words came quick and hard, each an angry blow to the boy's confidence. "Anyway, once you hold one in your arms, and it begins to soften into you, you'll not care for anything else."

The thought of this brought a smile to the boy's lips, but the girl did not see this because her torch was not pointing the right way. For several months, their village had been emerged in a blanket of darkness, ever since the sun had disappeared. But the boy wanted to express his happiness to her, so he took her free hand, and guided it towards his balled cheeks. "You're excited," she said, a statement, not a question. "Me too." She pulled her hand away and reached down for the cart rope which lay on the ground by her feet. "Come on. The sooner we find them, the sooner we can hold them."

"But," the boy shifted his weight from left foot to right, "seriously, don't you ever even consider where they come from?"

"Oh I don't know. Maybe someone from another village just turns up with a truckload. Your guess is as good as mine. But we have a map, so I guess we just call it a blessing and be grateful. Part of me thought we'd missed the boat." She shone her torch on his shoes and then let the triangle of white light fall on the dark path in front of them again. "Come," she said.

"Coming." He began to march after her. Adrenaline quicksilvered through his veins at the thought of what they might find.

They marched in silence through the dark of the day until the silence was broken by the girl. She stopped to speak. "If we do find the nearly babies—*when* we find them—we take as many as we can manage and give them all the love we have," she said.

"I guess," he mumbled. "I mean, I'd like to think that's what will happen. I have so much love to give, and no one else to give it too right now—" She began to stride forwards again with a renewed zest. Her feet made a pit pat sound on the firm mud and grass. He followed the girl, unsure as to whether he should offer to tow the empty cart up the dirt track away from the girl's father's hay barn where they'd met, or let her struggle onwards. "W-would—"

She stopped again and, this time, turned around. With the torch in her hand, she illuminated her face as if about to whisper a ghost story around a campfire. She groaned. "What is it? Spit it out."

"Doesn't matter."

"Listen. They probably die, the babies, if you don't give them enough love. You know that, right?" she said. "The nearly babes might die. If they're unloved, not held when they cry after they've been activated, we will have nothing left to hold and feed. And we can't let them die. We can't let anyone else get there first."

"There's nothing I'd like more than to hold one, nurture it for as long as it'll let me," the boy said. He bunched his fists into his pockets. He could just about make out the outline of a pebble by his foot under the light of the girl's torch. He kicked it away from the path. "I can't remember what it feels like to hold another breathing thing close. My mother hasn't touched me for weeks. I haven't seen another soul other than you in months." He sighed.

The girl flashed the beam in his eyes. "You and me both, bud. But don't go getting any ideas. And keep your greasy mitts off me." She dropped the rope of the cart, stepped towards him, and pointed to her upper middle cracked tooth. She moved in closer, so close he could smell the lack of care on her breath. He held his breath and turned his face away from hers. "This was how my father showed me love before him and my mother left with their new ones. Good riddance to parents, I say. Neither of them had time for me anyway, especially after their nearly babies arrived. My father didn't even take his beloved whisky bottles with him."

The girl knocked into the cart as she spoke and the cart began to trundle back down the slope. The boy stopped it with the side of his shin. He held in a yelp as the jagged wooden corner scraped against his leg.

"I know," he replied. "And I'm sorry. If it's any consolation, I haven't seen my mother since she got hers either. She hasn't even spoken to me. She took her nearly baby from the delivery man before I could even see it, let alone hold it, and now the only sound she makes is with her fist against her bedroom wall. She bangs and bangs on the wall until I slide her in bread and milk."

"Sucks to be you."

"I remember it crying once, the baby. It's screeching woke me on the fourth or fifth night after

116

it arrived. It cried for ages, and then it stopped. There was peace for a moment until Mother screamed. I haven't heard it cry since and ever since, Mother hasn't left her bedroom."

"Oh the sound of a nearly baby's crying is the worst. I guess."

"Yes. Yes it is."

The pair continued to walk.

***

"I think we're at the final crossroads," the girl said. She waved the beam of light ahead of them. The weak light bounced back: the tree they used to hang a rope swing from and play, before the darkness came, a sentinel oak bent like an old maid with a dowager's hump. "Yes, this is it. We're close."

The girl stopped and pulled out a folded sheet from the pocket of her dungaree dress. With three shakes, the map was open. She directed the torch beam onto the tatty paper and traced the route they'd need to take with her fingertip.

"The map," he asked. "You say the storekeeper gave it to you then ran back upstairs?"

"Correct. He'd said he was out of stock, said he was tired, and asked if I was certain it was what I wanted, a nearly baby," the girl said. "I visited his store every day for a fortnight, travelled there by torchlight, stubbed my toes on the journey more times than I care to remember."

"Paid off though, I guess," the boy said.

"I kept visiting, asking if he was expecting any more in. He must've grown tired of me bothering him. I'd ring the bell and each time he'd come down the stairs. No lights at all. No idea if he even had any clothes on or not. His stale smell filled the shop floor."

"Eew."

"He snapped at me, every time I called, said I'd wake his baby if I carried on ringing the bell. But I guess you're right. My persistence did pay off."

"Because he gave you the directions."

"Correct."

"And here we are," the boy said.

"And here we are." The girl passed the torch to the boy "Here, hold this. I think I know where to go now." she folded up the map and slid it back in her pocket. The torch flickered and dimmed in the boy's hand. "Dammit. It's running out." She took the torch back and pulled out new batteries from the satchel she wore over her body and replaced them. "Last lot," she said.

"Oh," the boy replied. "Guess we better get moving."

"Onwards. Into the woods."

They walked for another mile or so, around and through fields, until they reached the edge of the forest.

"Is it odd to not feel scared?" the boy said. "Or not as scared as I did when I came here once last year, before the sun went? In the dark, the forest feels the same as anywhere else."

"What you can't see can't scare you."

"You think? It's so quiet, as if all the wildlife has gone too," he said.

"Probably has. Nothing grows well without sunlight."

The boy shuddered. "Well it's certainly colder," he replied.

She agreed. Wrapped in perpetual darkness, the woods were no different to the rest of the village in which they resided. Bathed in black, they could not tell with their eyes where the field ended and where the thickness of trees began. Only with their hands and feet, it became apparent. "Come closer, so you don't stumble, the ground is uneven here, covered with some sort of bracken and darned twisted roots," she said. She dropped the tow rope of the cart and linked her arm through his. "We'll leave the cart here."

They didn't have to walk far until they heard the melody. "The babies are near," she said. "What a song. If all the black keys on the upright piano in the school hall were played in turn , softly, in an order never attempted before by any human, it wouldn't match the beauty of this music."

"It's...enchanting," he whispered.

The girl stopped and squeezed the boy in to her side a little closer. "But they never sing as sweetly again as they do before you hold them for the first time," she said. "Molly told me so. Before her father bought her one from the black market and she stopped coming to school."

Hand in hand, the two children crept towards the music, until a cluster of emerald eyes winking through the blanket of blackness brought them both to a standstill. "Have you ever seen such a beautiful shade of green?" she said and dropped the boy's hand. He was lost for words. She shone the torch beam onto the collection of babes and the melody escalated into high pitched screams. "Crikey," she said. "Sorry." He grabbed her torch and angled its beam towards the forest floor. The melody became pleasant again so the girl and the boy edged towards the thumb print swirl of blinking green lights.

"Like wood," he said. His sentence came out incomplete.

"Yes they are. Their skin, it's like knotted, polished timber—until you activate them."

The volume of the nearly babies increased as the girl passed the torch to the boy. "Here, take it," she said. He took the flashlight and she crouched down and lifted a singing babe up in her arms.

"You're so cold. There, there, my darling." She whispered into where its ear would form.

The boy placed the torch on the forest floor and followed suit, taking hold of the babe nearest him. "There there."

"This is unreal," she said quietly. "I never thought I'd get my own, and here we are. There are four, five including the one you're holding. All mine."

"Ours," he said.

"Yes. You can take one, these four need me."

He ran his fingertips over the nearly babe's hard outer casing. The green eye-lights twinkled like the stars the two children used to lie on the roof of the barn and gaze at.

"A true blessing. Those who wait the longest receive the most," she whispered. She placed and held her forefinger over each green eye of the babe in the crook of her arm until the eyes no longer glowed. If it weren't for the dim circle of yellow the

120

flashlight yielded, the girl and the babe would have sunken into the darkness of the wood completely. "Go ahead," she said, "activate yours too." The boy did as instructed. The girl held her babe close to her chest and then gathered up the others. Two were strewn on the forest floor and one was propped upright against a tree trunk. She held each close and activated it with her fingertip, then kissed each on where its forehead would develop.

As the last pair of green eye-lights went out, the sweet harmony stopped. The sound of their own breathing and the occasional crunch of leaf litter underfoot as they moved was all the two children could hear.

The boy picked up the torch from the ground, careful to support the fragile head of his baby as he did so. "I feel like a God," the girl said.

"A creator," the boy said. "They're so small. My heart might pop."

"The four of them together, I never knew I could feel so joyful," she said. "But my, they are weighty for their size. I daren't put them down." The girl rose up and took the boys hand and together, they walked back out of the forest towards where they'd left the cart.

"Let's leave the cart. Unless you want to use it?" she said. "We should head back to the barn and rest there until we've enough energy to take them back to our homes."

The wood-like skin of his babe had already started to soften, become more flesh-like. Undulating fronds where he presumed arm buds might swell tickled against his skin. "No. I don't

121

want to use the cart. I never want to put this one down."

"I feel them softening," she said. "They're gaining in weight too, already. I want to place them on my skin. Need to. But not here, not in the forest. It's too cold."

"Here," he said. He stretched out his arm. "Let me take one or two of yours. I can carry more weight. Just until we get back to the barn."

Before he had chance to touch one of the four babies in her arms, she snarled. The boy gasped. "Back off. Not a chance. These are mine. My babies. I got the map. So I get the lion's share."

"Sure," the boy said. He recoiled. "I'm sorry." He lifted his t-shirt up and placed his own baby against the skin of his chest. Instinct told him to do this. *Much easier to do with one than four,* he thought. He couldn't hold in the gasp of pure joy he felt as the wood began to moisten, soften off as it touched the smooth flesh of his chest. "One will be enough for me" he said. *Surely, one will be enough* he thought. He'd never felt such ecstasy. Pure, unfettered, unfiltered adoration for another thing. How could he want for anything more?

"Spring meadows, lemon balm." The girl inhaled her catch deeply and swayed with the scent. One of the young in her arms wriggled, then whimpered. She was taken aback and stumbled slightly. It was the first sound any of the babies had made since their sweet melody had stopped. A flashback to the brick-laden bag of kittens her uncle had made her carry to the river several years ago. "That was...different," she said.

122

"We must get going," the girl said, and with four babies, each softening slightly in her arms, each moulding and contorting its wet willow limbs inwards and around her waist and chest to find its special place with its new mother, she turned to exit the forest. "Come on, I need you to shine the way." One of her yield released another uncomfortable murmur. She cooed. The soothing nature of her voice calmed the fidgeting bundle in her arms. She cooed all the walk back.

***

"Please, let me in," the boy rapped on the front door of the girl's house. He'd lost track of how many days it had been since their journey into the woods. He must have closed his eyes for a split second, exhausted from caring for his baby, and his babe, strapped to his chest with its own limb buds, had started to cry. He knocked again, harder. He needed to get into the warmth of the girl's house so he could unswaddle the baby in order to begin the tedious stroking ritual the little one demanded. He reached down and felt his leg gently. He'd tripped on his way, in the dark, to the girl's house, despite its proximity to his. The graze on his knee burnt.

Caring for the baby was hard enough, despite the lack of light. His mother had taken the last of the candles into her room before she took up residence there. The boy had reached breaking point, alone in the dark with the fresh wood-baby, so he left his house to the sound of his mother banging the wall of her bedroom. This was her demand for food, but there was nothing left in the kitchen to give her and he had spiked his hand hard on a broken glass jar while rummaging in the back of the larder.

His decision to head over to the girl's house had not come easy—he was a little afraid of how she would react to his neediness—but he wanted to know what he had witnessed was normal, and he wanted to find out the best way to cope. And the girl next door always had answers.

"Get in." The girl opened the door. A row of candles on a plinth in her hallway flickered and rippled with the draft as she did so. He squinted at the brightness of her entrance room. "You look how I feel," he said.

"Exhausted?" she replied. "I haven't slept for days, not since we got back from the barn."

"Same." The boy followed the girl through. Despite the weariness he felt, despite questioning his own sanity at times, to be in her presence, in the presence of another not made from softened wood or cursed with the piercing cry of a banshee, was what he needed. And to be in a room with light again, after so long in the darkness of his own abode, felt better. He exhaled audibly and she waived him through to her living room where he sank into a wicker cup chair.

"Here. Breakfast." The girl passed him a muffin. "It's stale but its sustenance. The weight has fallen off you."

"Thank you. And same. I see your collar bone." He took a bite. His empty stomach curled with the arrival of the solid food. Slowly. He would need to eat it slowly in order to not vomit. He placed the cake down on a table at his side and began the

124

laborious process of untying his baby from his chest.

"They don't come away easily, do they?" she said and lifted her shirt. The boy, for the first time, was glad at the dimness of the lighting. Myriad leather-like digits and limbs probed and hustled for skin space on the girl's bruised-blue torso. She stroked what he considered might be the spine of one of her babes and she cooed weakly. "There there," she said. He turned away, unable to watch.

"No." He prized what he presumed were the lips of his nearly babe from a raised mole on his stomach with the firm slip of his pinky and began to peel away the rest of the baby from his chest. The girl strode around the room, in a repeating circuit, caressing each of her young ones in turn.

"I want you to watch something," he said. "I need to know if this is happening to you too."

"Go ahead," she said. She turned to face the boy then continued to rock in rhythm with her own gentle cooing and hushing.

The boy laid his baby down flat on the edge of the rug which lay in between him and the girl. His near-babe began to whimper, then cry, then scream. The boy gripped the arms of his chair tightly. "I want to pick it up again. I've an overwhelming urge to tend to it, make it feel loved, safe, but I'm empty inside. Tired out. Every part of me aches. The lack of sleep, the constant soothing, it's too much." He spoke louder as the sound of his baby amplified.

"Make it stop," she shouted. Several of her babes, all strapped around her waist and sides, all in awkward positions, burst into tears. The boy's babe screamed louder. "I never let mine cry so loud," she snapped. Her eyes widened until, even in the dim light, the boy could see their whites.

"Please," he said, his hands clamped, prayer position in front of his chest. "Please, just wait."

The shrill sound from his baby grew and grew. Louder. Louder. Until it stopped. "Look," he said. "Its cheeks." His nearly baby on the floor, part knotted-wood, part frilly pink-white tissue, inhaled deeply through the gash on its top half. The two children watched on as the babe's cheeks puffed out.

"What is it doing?" she said. "Help it!" She wrapped her arms tight around her own collection of babes and kissed each one on where its fully formed head would grow.

"This. This happened yesterday. I couldn't take any more, couldn't hold it any longer. Its suction slit found my nipples. Look at them!" The boy lifted his shirt up and moved towards the lamp at his side. The girl gasped. "They're red raw. I bled, it bit on me so hard. And believe me, I wanted to let it carry on, because, for a moment, it seemed content, at peace, but it hurt. It hurt so much." He dropped his shirt, buckled forward in his seat and cried.

"I don't know what to say. You just have to keep on loving it. Love it with all you have in your heart. You can do it. What do they say, the days are long but the years are short." She paused and prized away one of her own babe's wooden spindles which had begun to search upwards for her breast. "Ouch. And they won't be babies forever." She reached forward and patted the boy on the knee, then brushed her hand against his face, wiping a tear from his cheek.

"I know. I'm trying. Believe me. It fills me with an unmatchable happiness when it eventually pulls its roots out from my flesh and unclamps its slit and dozes against my skin. But I'm so tired. I swear I'm delusional. That's why I came here. I need you to see this too."

"The breath-holding?" The girl tilted her head, looked down at the baby on the floor. "It must be some sort of protest. It's unhappy you've removed it and placed it on the floor, surely. Who can blame it?"

"Yes. That may well be the case. But that's not all, the breath-holding," he said. "Watch." He gestured with a limp wrist and pointed finger at his babe on the floor without looking up. "Please."

She crouched down by the side of his baby, drew her nose closer to the now tight slit at the top of the bundle of knots and softness, and observed.

"It's turning blue," she said, flustered. "I need to pick it up, please, let me touch your child. This is unbearable, watching it puff out its cheeks like this. I swear, the place where its face will form is swelling, growing. Its unhappiness is unsettling my babes. My youngest is arching." She pointed to the baby draped over her left shoulder. "And this one here, on my hip, the first one I activated, its writhing, pulsing almost, like it feels the pain of yours. You can't leave yours here on the ground. Please, before it attaches—pick it up. Look—it's putting out roots into the floor boards, see?"

127

"Please, be patient. Place your fingers in your ears, coo. Just wait and watch."

But she couldn't resist helping it. Mother's instinct. With a gentle hand, she caressed the side of part of its top. The roots the babe had laid down flash-recoiled and the girl yanked her hand away in shock and fell back. The nearly babe on the floor opened up its slit and sucked in a large volume of air through its pre-mouth gash. The babe swelled up more, inflated. Its barky flesh stretched and widened, and it became globular in shape until the whole babe had tripled in size.

"Please, pick it up," she said. "It won't let me touch it." Her finger stung where she had tried to soothe the boy's babe.

"Just watch," the boy said. He was not watching. His face was firmly planted in the palms of his hands.

His babe slowly lifted off from the ground, until eventually no part of it touched the rug or the floor boards. "It's floating," she screamed. Her babies matched her volume. She ran out into the hallway.

The boy looked up. *It wasn't a delusion,* he thought. *They float.* The baby's cheek pads puffed out further and further and it rose up like a light balloon until it hovered midway between the floor and the ceiling. "Look at its skin. Gone blue," he said. "When you ignore them, leave them to cry, they hold their breath until they float. I just needed someone else to witness it, to know I'm not going mad."

128

"Just take it back into your arms, where it's supposed to be," she yelled. "Please. Take it back or get out."

"Yes. Of course. You're right. I need to hold it again. That feeling when they sleep on your chest. Nothing beats it." The boy sprung up then he just stood statuesque, as if tethered to the spot. "But I'm so tired of holding it. Alone in that dark house, with no food, with what might as well be the ghost of my mother banging on her bedroom wall, giving all her love to another bundle. Who holds me, who soothes me?"

"Your nearly baby gives you all the love you'll ever need," she said. "The slit, take it and angle the slit on your nipple again, please. Breathe through the discomfort. Endless giving, it's what a parent should do for their baby, in return for unconditional love."

"But it's not my baby," he whispered. Quietly enough for her not to hear. "It's not even a baby." He looked to his feet then walked slowly towards the door.

"You can't leave it with me, I have four of my own, they give me all I need. I've nothing left to give another. Besides, yours won't even let me touch it." The girl marched towards the boy and pushed in front of him, her weak body working as a shield to the door to block him from leaving.

"And I need light. I can't bear to live in darkness any longer. You have so much light here and I have nothing." The boy seized the opportunity and grabbed a lantern from the cabinet by the girl's front door.

129

"If you're not going to love it, at least take it with you. Please don't leave it here, it takes up so much space. And what if it stops holding its breath and starts to cry again? Please, take it away with you." The girl lurched forwards, away from the door, and grabbed the floating nearly babe by one of its unfurled limbs. "Please take it away." The boy pushed past her, towards the open door and stepped outside. The girl pushed his baby after him but he refused to hold onto it.

The boy's baby opened up its slit and took in a large gasp of air and grew larger. The skin which held it together stretched out so thin, it became translucent in patches. A muffled blue hue shone from within it which illuminated it.

"That's new," the boy said. He pointed at his baby. "That light within it." A pang of fresh love struck his heart and he reached out, shoulder height, to touch his baby. "Perhaps I can tolerate it a little longer. Maybe it will get easier to care for as it grows." The blue light within the baby flickered off and on and off and on. The boy grappled after it, jumped and tried to reach for it back, but in a matter of seconds, the ball of nearly baby had risen up higher and became out of his reach.

Too high. It floated upwards, far out of his reach. It drifted out of the door and rose up and out of the girl's house. As it came into contact with the cool external air, the blue light within the baby disappeared completely. Much like the sun had all those months ago. But the boy and the girl could still see the baby, despite the darkness. Its taut skin reflected the light of the lantern. The boy lifted the lantern and stood and watched as the babe-orb inhaled and inhaled, increased in diameter, and rose up and up.

The boy and the girl could make out its flailing oaky limbs which began to kick and bend and the nearly baby swam up higher, into the dark sky.

With their necks flexed back, the children stared up until the boy's baby became a dot up in what, despite its hellish, lightless nature, must've been the morning summer sky. They squinted. The boy cried. A sadness greater than the dark sky which stretched above him yanked at his heart, pulled him to an even more bleak place than the Earth had become since the sun had appeared to have taken its final breath. A misery with more depth than the author sharing this tale with you may have felt, when perchance, once she herself had become embalmed with the despair of watching on helpless, as her nearly-babe took one final breath in her arms and never a second.

The girl cried too. "Angle the lantern in such a way so we can see your baby," she said through sobs. They watched up, up, as it drifted further from her house. The girl gasped. "Look," she said, her voice louder.

The boy's baby, a small orb reflecting the light of the lantern in an otherwise black landscape, bumped into another small flailing-limbed ball. Both children squinted. "Another inflated baby," the girl said. "I can make out your nearly-babe, there," she pointed with the lantern in her outstretched arm, "and another baby there, see, at its side." And she was correct. They watched on in awe as the boy's

131

babe nudged another baby, which Newton's cradled a cluster of other inflated, wood-skinned balls.

The two children shrieked. A sharp beam of sunlight broke through the blackness and singed the children's retinas, as the bunch of floating babies rippled to the side. The boy closed his eyes. A staggered rainbow of the outline of his own darling inflated baby imprinted onto the inside of his eyelid.

"The sun," he said, his voice reedy, desperate, dry with exhaustion. He rubbed his eyes then opened them again. "Up there. In front of the sun, the darkness is nothing but a thick cloud of inflated nearly babies, lifting upwards, towards the heavens."

In a split second, the sunshine burst disappeared, became clouded over again, and, as if on cue, the lantern supped up the last of its kerosene and dipped out. Side by side, the boy and the girl and everything else in existence became immersed once more in darkness, lost to the eternal heartbreak of the midnight of summer.

On her breast, one of the girl's nearly babies began to stir, then, despite her efforts to soothe it, it broke into a cry. With the cup of her hand, the girl clasped the place where she worried the head of her babe might form. On the spot, she rocked slightly, a little broken, the way new mothers do what seems like forevermore when soothing a precious one. "There, there," she said. She placed her lantern on the ground and with her spare hand, she reached across and fumbled in the darkness until she found him. She patted the crown of the head of the weeping boy. On the rough, long, unseen grass outside of the house in which the girl would spend the rest of her life, the boy had fallen to his knees. His face was, once more, pressed into his palms. "There, there."

Sweet Jane (Thomas M. Malafarina)

"I'm on the path to being someone I'm equally terrified by and obsessed with. My true self." - Troye Sivan

"I was terrified to be my true self because I felt that it wasn't enough. But I allowed myself to break down those walls." - Hannah Brown

"I yam what I am, and dat's all dat I yam." – Popeye the Sailor

1

The rain beat down on the roof of the new Lexus RX 500, sounding like the thundering hooves of a dozen stallions. The night was dark and miserable, with his county in the midst of one of the worst storms they had seen in a decade or more. The local weather service called for several inches of rainfall and warned of potential flash flooding. Paul Stoddard couldn't wait to get his new wheels out of the storm and into the safety of his garage.

Paul supposed he should be grateful there was no hale to accompany this storm. The last thing he wanted to deal with was hale damage on his new car's finish, especially since he had busted his butt for the past several years to be able to afford this baby. It had been a good financial year for him, and now this latest promotion from regional to national sales manager had been just the boost his bank account needed.

"Paul Stoddard, national sales manager," Paul said aloud to himself in the privacy of his new car. "Yeah, baby! You know it!" He shouted as he smacked his fist triumphantly against the steering wheel. He was still trying to wrap his head around this latest promotion. As confident as he sounded, Paul had been experiencing his typical mixed emotions about his new responsibilities. He was, of course, proud of his promotion and thrilled with the salary increase. However, he was also apprehensive and perhaps a bit insecure about his abilities to handle the job.

Fortunately, he recognized these emotions from the many other times he had to deal with them while climbing the corporate ladder. Now, at the ripe old age of fifty, his hard work was financially beginning to pay off in dividends. He knew, eventually, he'd find a way to work past these feelings of uncertainty. In the end, he would most certainly succeed as he always had. He was Paul Stoddard, dammit, and that meant he could do anything. Hell, he already had.

As the car traveled along the slick country two-lane, Paul made certain to avoid as many of the numerous water-filled potholes in the road as possible while simultaneously keeping alert for deer. Two things you could always count on along Central Pennsylvania highways were potholes and deer. He looked up ahead and could hardly believe his eyes. Someone was standing out there by the roadside in the pouring rain with their thumb extended, looking for a ride. As he got closer, he saw a long, lean leg leading up to a short skirt and realized the hitchhiker was a young woman.

Despite the dismal weather, Paul was feeling good today, and as his momentary doubts about his abilities began to fade, he experienced a resurgence of confidence, although perhaps overconfidence would be a better description. He decided to play the knight in $65,000 worth of shining armor in the form of rolling steel and rescue this damsel in distress. Who knows? Maybe if she was impressed with him, it could lead to a little sumpin-sumpin, as they say. He assumed the woman might be a bit "loose" regarding the morals department. Why else would she be out here, thumbing a ride on a dark, miserable night such as this.

Suddenly, Paul imagined dozens of sexual fantasies ala Penthouse Magazine that flashed through his mind as he pulled the car over to the shoulder and opened the door for the woman.

2

"Please, come in out of that horrible weather," Paul called over the noise of the storm.

The young woman ducked into the car, sat on the seat, and immediately apologized, "I'm so sorry for all the water I'm getting in your beautiful car."

"Don't worry about it." Paul said, "It'll dry."

She looked Paul in the eye and said, "That's so sweet and considerate of you. Thank you, by the way, for the ride."

Paul was taken aback by her eyes. Those eyes seemed incredible, radiating a light that appeared to

136

cross the distance between them and wrap itself around his soul like a lasso. He realized how ridiculous that thought was, but it was how he felt.

"N ... no ... no problem," Paul stammered, "Happy to help. So, um ... where are you heading?"

She smiled a million-dollar Hollywood smile and said, "Nowhere in particular. I suppose I'm heading wherever you're going." There was that mischievous look again, "I'll see what adventure awaits me at the end of the line."

Again, Paul found himself captivated by this mysterious and incredibly sensual young woman. To call her a young woman was a bit of a stretch; physically, she appeared more like a girl. Paul guessed she couldn't be much more than eighteen years old. "Legal or San Quentin quail?" He wondered, then mentally chastised himself for having such a thought.

"Sounds like you're something of a free spirit," Paul said, feeling like the fantasies he had been imagining might have a shot at becoming a reality. How did those stories in Penthouse Forum all seem to start? "You may not believe this happened to me. I can hardly believe it myself..."

She chuckled and agreed, "Oh yes, you could most definitely call me that."

"Oh, by the way, I'm Paul, Paul Stoddard." He said as he extended his right hand for a shake, not expecting what followed.

The woman took it, gave his hand a gentle caress that sent shockwaves of sensuality surging through his body, and said, "I'm Jane Sweetwater, but people just call me Sweet Jane."

Paul's throat felt dry, and he wasn't sure he could put together two sensible words to reply. To distract himself, Paul checked for oncoming traffic and, seeing none, pulled out onto the highway. Then he gulped, tried to find moisture in his mouth, and asked, "Sweet Jane? You mean ... like the Lou Reed song?"

"Yeah, that old guy. My parents were big fans of his. I guess that's why they always called me Sweet Jane. Were you a Lou Reed fan?"

"No, not really. I knew who he was. I was something of an amateur musician back in the day, but I wasn't really into that whole New York and New Wave scene. You know, bands like Lou Reed and the Velvet Underground, The New York Dolls, the Ramones; not my thing."

"They were all before my time. I don't know any of those names except for Lou Reed. You know, because of my folks."

Paul remembered that at fifty years old, he was old enough to be this girl's father. He suddenly felt dirty for having the thoughts he had earlier. His own daughter was not much older than this girl, but unlike Sweet Jane, she was safely tucked away in her junior year of college.

He said, "Um ... if you don't mind my asking ... I mean ... you seem kinda young to be ... you know ... out thumbing a ride ... on a night like this, out here in the middle of nowhere."

She smiled and said, "I'm nineteen. And I've been doing this for a long time, so you don't have to worry about me. Although it's sweet of you to be concerned. Usually, no one is."

138

In a brief moment of moonlight breaking through the gloom, Paul noticed a dark expression cloud Sweet Jane's young face, momentarily cracking her easy-going facade, and he realized by that brief look this girl had experienced more than anyone so young should have. He thought again of his daughter, and a new wave of shame passed over him. If his ex-spouse knew what he had been thinking earlier, Paul would have been given him an earful. Then again, he was always given an earful; that's part of the reason for the title "ex."

Paul asked, "You mentioned your parents earlier. How do they feel about you ... you know, traveling about like this ... alone?"

"They don't feel anything ... they're dead."

Paul was stunned again. He hadn't expected that. He said, "Oh ... I'm so sorry ... I didn't... I mean, I never ..."

"Don't sweat it, Paul. It was a long time ago, back when I was fourteen. I've had years to deal with it. I'm ok now." She put her hand on Paul's thigh, much closer to his crotch than his knee.

Again, his throat began to feel dry as electricity pulsed through him.

"So, um ... if I may ask ... what happened to your folks? Were they in a car accident or something like that?"

Sweet Jane's voice took on a more somber and monotone quality as she said, "No, Paul. Nothing like that. They were both murdered."

3

Paul grabbed tighter to the steering wheel, shocked by Sweet Jane's revelation and certain he would lose control of his car. When he could think coherently again, he said, "Did you say … murdered?"

Still, in that same matter-of-fact monotone, she replied, "Yes, they were stabbed to death in their sleep with a butcher knife from our kitchen while I was in the bedroom down the hall from them. I heard their dying screams."

"Oh my god! That's terrible! What an awful thing to have to go through." Then he realized something and said, "You were lucky to have survived. Did you hide under your bed, in a closet, or climb out a window?"

"No, nothing like that. I just pulled the covers over my head and went back to sleep. That's where the police found me when they arrived. I'm told a neighbor called them after hearing my parents screaming."

Paul felt like a thousand worms were crawling under his skin. This was one of the most horrible stories he had ever heard, and hearing it from this young girl in that strange, detached tone only made it seem worse.

"So what happened? Did they catch the killer?"

Jane sighed and said, "No, the police never found out who did it."

"I'm so sorry to hear that, Jane. Such an awful and traumatic thing to go through at such a young age."

"It was what it was, and I managed to move on."

"So what happened to you after that? I mean, did you go into the foster care system?"

"No ... well, not at that time. I was turned over to my Dad's brother, Mark, my uncle, and his wife, Lenore. They lived in another state and had a young son, Bobby, who was a few years older than me."

"So, that was a good thing, right? I mean, you were with family. That's gotta be better than with strangers."

"You would think so, and in the beginning, everything worked out pretty good ... until ..."

Paul asked, "Until what?"

Jane's voice seemed to get even more distant when she said, "Well, I feel a bit funny sharing this with a stranger, but ... things were ok until Uncle Mark and Cousin Bobby started making late-night visits to my bedroom."

Paul knew where this story was heading, "On no, Jane. Are you saying ..."

"Yeah, they raped and sodomized me nightly. Aunt Lenore knew what was happening but did nothing about it. Some nights she even sat on a chair watching them, you know, do sick stuff to me. She even got in on the fun twice and molested me while they watched."

"Oh my god! That's terrible. Did you go to the police or maybe a teacher or minister for help?"

"No, Paul, I couldn't. I was a stranger in their town; they were well-known and respected. Mark was even active in his church leadership. Aunt Lenore volunteered for school events, and Bobby was his class's president. I was just some discarded piece of trash dumped on them."

"I'm so sorry, Jane. How long did you have to deal with ... with the abuse?"

"Luckily, not long. There was a tragic fire, and the house burned to the ground. Uncle Mark, Aunt Lenore, and Cousin Bobby all died in the fire. I was the only survivor."

"Sounds to me like they got what they deserved," Paul said, although he couldn't help but notice the strange coincidence that this unusual young woman had managed to avoid death twice.

Jane didn't reply.

"So what happened after that?"

She said, "I was shipped off to my father's Aunt Sarah, my great Aunt."

4

"She was really old, like in her eighties. She was half-crippled and bonkers in the head, you know?"

"You mean she was senile?"

"Big time. Aunt Sarah didn't know who I was most of the time. She thought I was her kid or something, which was weird since she was never married and had no kids. I guess it's strange how you get when your brain starts to go ..."

Although it was mostly dark in the car, Paul could see Jane making circular motions with her finger around her ear, the universal sign for crazy. She said, "If I hadn't been able to care for myself, I probably would have starved to death. I ended up taking care of her most of the time. She often crapped herself too. Not a fun experience, I'm telling you."

Paul said, "That was nice of you to care for her. I assume she eventually passed away."

"Yep. She did a header down a flight of steps and broke her neck along with a bunch of other bones. And before you ask, I was not sent to live with any other relatives. I guess we ran out of takers. I was put into the system, which bounced me from one abusive home to another until I ran away when I was sixteen, and I've been on my own ever since."

"You poor thing," Paul said, "How tragic. It seems you've been through so much."

Jane said, "I have. Yet here I am, stronger than ever."

Paul sighed, then said, Look, Jane, I'm going to suggest something ... and I hope it doesn't sound weird or anything ... and there's no catch ... I expect nothing in return."

"What is it, Paul?" Jane asked, but she already knew what he was going to suggest. She always knew.

"You see, I'm divorced, and my daughter, Cindy, is away at college. I have a big house all to myself. If you would like, you could spend the night. You can get a nice shower, and I can cook you a delicious dinner. You are welcome to sleep in my daughter's room and borrow some of her clothes while I run those wet things through the washer and dryer."

Jane was quiet momentarily, then slipped her hand up toward Paul's crotch and said, "That all

143

sounds fantastic, but I have to find some way to pay you for your kindness."

Paul gently pushed her hand aside and said, "I appreciate the offer, but there is no need. You have been through so much; I cannot, in good conscience, take advantage of you like that. Allow me to just help you tonight, and tomorrow you can be on your way if that's your wish."

Jane slowly pulled her hand away, unsure of what to make of this stranger. She said, "Ok, Paul. I accept."

Paul thought he saw a strange expression cross Jane's face in the moonlight. It was one that momentarily sent chills racing down his spine.

5

Later that night, after Jane had dinner, she was relaxing on the sofa dressed in a pair of Paul's daughter's pajamas. A crime drama was playing on the television; Jane was hardly paying attention to the show as she was a bit troubled. Paul had been so kind to her, much more considerate than she deserved, yet she knew who and what she was, and nothing could change that.

"So, what are we watching?" Paul asked as he walked into the family room carrying Jane's recently washed, dried, and folded clothes.

Jane said, "I don't know. Some cop show. Not sure which one, but it doesn't really matter anyway. They're all pretty much the same."

"Yeah, I get what you mean. Did you ever notice how on TV the cops always manage to catch the murderer in an hour, but in the real world, people get away with murder all the time?"

Jane hesitated momentarily, wondering what Paul was getting at, then said, "Yeah. I pretty sure everybody wonders about that, but that's just, you know, TV." Actually, she had never thought that and was a bit concerned why Paul would bother asking her such a thing. She now knew what she had to do.

"Well, Jane. It's late, I had a very busy, and I must say, interesting day. I'm going to bed now, and I'll see you in the morning. I think you'll sleep well in Cindy's bed tonight. Goodnight, Sweet Jane."

Again, Jane was caught off guard by the kindness this man offered her, and he expected nothing in return. She wished he had treated her badly or demanded sex or something to justify her actions. But then again, he did show signs of suspicion. Regardless, she had no choice, so later this night she would murder Paul Stoddard in his sleep.

6

Paul heard the door to his bedroom slowly opening as he sat upright in the darkness, waiting for Sweet Jane to come to him, not as the mysterious woman of his sexual fantasies but as the serial killer he knew she really was. And, as he suspected, Sweet Jane had not let him down.

She stood silhouetted in the now open doorway to Paul's bedroom, backlit by the nightlight in the hallway. He could see something long and pointed in her hand and knew it was a butcher's knife from the wood block in his kitchen.

In as calm a voice as he could manage, Paul asked, "So, Sweet Jane. This is how you repay my kindness, by killing me in my sleep like you murdered your parents so many years ago?"

"I never said I killed them, Paul. But yeah … you're right. I did stab them to death, and I burned Uncle Mark's house down, and I pushed that senile old bitch down the stairs."

"My guess is there have been others you have killed as well," Paul said from the darkness.

"Yes. Many others."

"And now you plan to kill me, someone whose only mistake was being kind to you. Care to explain why?"

Jane said, "I'm not sure I understand either. I suppose it's just who I am, just how I'm wired. I'm not doing this because it's fun or exciting or because I get some sort of thrill from it. I just do it because I have to."

"You may be surprised to know, I understand," Paul replied.

"You do?" Jane exclaimed. "But how can you understand?"

"I just do." Paul said, "It's not because of how your parents treated you or your subsequent abusive experiences. You see, Sweet Jane, you are truly an unusual commodity. Female serial killers are very rare. They are few and far between. However, I pegged you as one right from the start."

Jane was puzzled, "But how did you know?"

"I suppose it takes one to know one, as they say," Paul replied heartily.

Jane was confused, "Takes one to know one? That makes no sense. I don't understand. You're not a serial killer; even if you were, you're not a woman."

Although Jane could not see Paul in the darkness, she could tell by his voice he was smiling as he spoke the next shocking words. He said, "No, not a woman anymore."

7

Jane was stunned to silence for a beat, eventually finding her voice, "What are you saying? You said you had a daughter and were divorced from ... from your wife."

"Not true, sweet, Sweet Jane. I said spouse; I never used the word wife. If I had ever referred to my husband, I would have been careful to say spouse, not husband."

Jane gripped her knife more tightly and took a single step across the doorway's threshold. She was becoming more uncomfortable by the minute. This was not going at all as she had planned. She decided the best thing to do was to keep this freak distracted long enough to get within stabbing distance.

She said, "So you're telling me you were a woman once, as well as a wife and mother?" She took another small step forward and heard a clicking sound she recognized as a gun getting ready to fire.

"That's far enough, Sweet Janie," Paul said as he clicked on the reading light on the end table beside his bed. When her eyes adjusted, Jane saw Paul pointing a large caliber handgun directly at her. She didn't know enough about weapons to determine the gun's ability to inflict damage because she had never used firearms. But based on the size of the hole in the barrel, she decided that the hand cannon most definitely could do some major damage.

Paul said, "In answer to your question, yes, I was a woman, a wife, and a mother. In fact, I gave birth to our daughter, Cindy. I tried to be a good wife and do the whole family thing. But ... well, unfortunately, I, too, was a female serial killer. I had over a dozen kills before transitioning to a male and another six after that. And you, Sweet Jane, will be my seventh."

Big Bottle, Little Bottles (Stuart Holland)

Have you ever walked through a graveyard at night when there is no moon and the air is cold? If you have, did you perhaps pause for a moment, lingering to look at the latest gravestone, wondering what was down there, six feet under your feet? Did you even smell the acrid, pungent aroma of the decaying body beneath you? No? Why not?

They call me "Stinky" where I come from. It's not because I don't wash, I do, every morning when I rise and every night when I have put my bottles away. The trouble is the bottles. It's why I live alone with the greatest of secrets. For I am the designated spirit catcher in my area, one of hundreds so assigned by our master, a veritable army of spirit catchers sent by our lord and master on one of the most onerous tasks you can imagine. Let me freeze your bones as I explain my task here on this mortal coil.

I became a spirit catcher by accident just over twenty-five years ago. It was a near-death moment as my shattered body waited interminably for the ambulance people to scoop me off the road where I had become a victim of a road traffic accident. To be fair, I don't think my pushbike had much chance against the idiot in the massive lorry that swerved into my path. But I survived and as I sensed the dark shadow hovering above me, sickle in hand, I did a deal – my life if I served him. And that's how I got my job.

My job is to visit cemeteries by day and graveyards in the dead of night. I perform a thankless task, if truth be told, but it is essential.

Maybe I should explain something. We all have a spirit lurking somewhere under our skin. That spirit is trapped for all the time we are alive on this miserable planet. Okay you may think it's a great planet but honestly if it wasn't for people like me, it would soon become a desperate place to be. You see, the spirit within needs feeding just as we need feeding. If it's not fed the right way, it festers, rots and turns evil. And since there are SO many people around these days, the feeding thing has become a problem. Actually, it became a problem a hundred or so years ago. Now, when you die, two things happen. First your physical body rots, which is bad enough. But the second thing is the body eventually releases its spirit and it is this which is the real problem. Billions upon billions of spirits have now been released into the air and they are clogging up the feeding process of the living spirits in people's bodies. Now, it transpires about one percent of spirits are released at the point of death or within an hour, roughly. The overwhelming majority are not. I do not know why, but they are what we in the business call retained spirits. They will be released, several days later or even a year. The most likely is they will be released at the first sign of increased heat at the crematorium, but if the body is to be buried it can take months for the heat of decomposition to cause the release.

So, to cut a very long story into something more manageable, my job has become to capture these spirits when they are released. It requires dedication, perseverance and a fairly hefty chunk of luck. Let's look at the two most common scenarios. The first is the retained spirit in the crematorium scenario. You can picture the scene – a group of mourners gathered outside the building as their loved one has passed beyond the curtain and on towards the fiery furnace (which the public never sees as it would be too distressing). Even as the gathered mourners share a few anecdotes before leaving the crematorium for the wake, a cloud of faint white smoke can be seen emanating from the top of the chimney stack. This is my moment. I hover in the background, unseen, always unseen. When I know there will be smoke, I take my little bottle from my coat pocket and remove the stopper. Next I have a small musical instrument which makes a sound a bit like wind. I turn it on with one hand and wait until I feel the spirit pass out of the top of the chimney and float downwards to the sound. By carefully positioning the bottle in a certain way, I have learned to capture the spirit. Rarely the spirit will fight back and cause problems, and occasionally it has been so determined to elude the bottle I have had to let it go. Usually though, the spirit is grateful for its new home, at least for the moment, so I can put the stopper back in the bottle and walk away nonchalantly from the scene, the spirit now trapped in my possession until I can hand it over to the master.

Of course, crematoriums are busy places so I actually carry around several of these little, stoppered bottles. Each one starts off sealed, and I have to break that seal to remove the stopper, so I can never accidentally release one spirit while capturing another.

The other part of my job is dealing with the retained spirits that are physically buried. This is often down to luck as much as anything. To capture a buried, retained spirit is not actually that different to capturing a spirit in a crematorium. The process entails me walking through a graveyard, often when the air is cold and the night is dark. Not many spirits give themselves up from the ground in daylight, I have found. Using the same little instrument I walk around the graveyard looking at the recent committals (they are easy to identify as the ground is piled up and has not yet settled as if it has never been disturbed), using my little instrument with a bottle at the ready. I never know who or what is going to come to the weird, almost ethereal, sound, but come they do. Most nights when I go out, something comes to me. Sometimes it is more than one. I suppose you might say I am lucky in that there are a handful of graveyards in the area where I live, so I can easily keep an eye on daytime activity, and return under the cover of darkness until I have received the retained spirits that have decided to reveal themselves.

My work done for the day I can eventually return to my flat. It's not ostentatious, more functional, but it does have two bedrooms. Before I can relax I have one more task to perform and I do that in the spare bedroom. Each little bottle I have used this day must be placed on the table, one at a time. There is a bigger bottle waiting and carefully, oh so carefully, I have to open the little bottle so the spirit can be transferred to the bigger bottle. I have no idea how this magic works but work it does, every time. When I have carefully emptied all the little bottles into the bigger one, I screw down the lid of the bigger bottle. I leave it on the table, and discard the little bottles in my regular recycling bin. I then leave the skylight window to the spare bedroom open a small amount, close the door and relax.

Sometime during the night the window will open and the bottle will be taken and a new, empty one put in its place, with the screw lid placed by its side. When my supply of the little bottles runs low I find the next day a fresh supply is waiting for me. I have learned that these little bottles are for single use only. Which is why they come to me sealed and why, once I have captured a spirit and then transferred it to the bigger bottle, the little ones have to be recycled. If I didn't do that by now my flat would be overrun with bottles and that would never do.

How long will I have to perform this thankless, but vital, task, you may ask. The answer is I have no idea, but I suspect it will be until shortly before my own spirit is captured by another spirit catcher. Oh, and in case you are wondering, I have long ago planned for my own cremation. The thought of having six feet of dirt on top of me does not interest me at all.

The Last Resort (Liam A. Spinage)

It is not easy writing this message. I have lived a life of privilege, free of guilt, free of consequence. It is only in the events of the last few hours that each of these has caught up with me and forced me to witness the true horrors of my actions.

I do not seek forgiveness, for I know now that is beyond me. I know my fate. My only hope is that whosoever should find this should learn from the error of my ways and therefore that my death may have more meaning than my life. I go now willingly, but not before I pen this dire warning to those of a similar calling or possessed of like ideas. You will bring this place, all places, to utter ruin and destruction in your futile pursuits. Stop now before it is too late.

If that warning is insufficient, if you demand evidence, then allow me to attach a name and a story to it so that the world may come to understand the folly of my life and the manner of my execution. Read on and weep, by all means, but take heed of the lessons within. These lessons are for us all.

I am known to the world as 'Captain' Yiannis Xiphias, shipping magnate, owner of fleets of commercial ships and ocean liners. It is typical among us monied folk to indicate that our wealth is a well-deserved reward for a lifetime of hard work. My own life differs considerably from this narrative, and I make no claim to it: it is common enough knowledge in the biographies in glossy magazines that I was a jobbing deckhand who just happened to be close enough to save a drowning heiress from a watery grave. When romance ensued from gratitude, her father cared not that I was poor, only that I was clearly a man of the sea.

Thus, catapulted into both fame and fortune, my life changed immeasurably for the better. Previous friends were treated with the professional aloofness befitting my new status as their ultimate boss. The crew I'd served with became distant and in their place the yachting set embraced me with open arms. I moved in different circles, learning the old man's business with his daughter on my arm. I expanded the operations rapidly and confidently. Our cruise liners were packed with eager sightseers, swooping on every Mediterranean port, flocking to bazaars and churches, museums and galleries, keen to have a quick fix of cultures they could take home and place on their mantelpieces as mementos. I latched onto each new venture with the arrogant swagger of someone who had it all but always wants more and will do anything to get it.

It was early February when my yacht Helen's Joy rounded the coast and drew close to the haunting beauty of La Serenissima, that ancient and marvellous city of Venice where I had hoped to meet with like-minded company to enjoy the celebrations of the annual carnival. I should have noticed first that something was amiss, when the air and the waters alike were enveloped in a low, lingering fog rather than the brilliance of the late winter sunshine which habitually greeted us at this time of year. The light in Venice always visits twice - first from the sun and then from boundless reflections on the canals which have lent a quiet beauty and elegance to the city from time immemorial.

We drew in toward the docks which came up before us in eerie silence. I could spot masked figures waiting for us at the quayside, cowled and cloaked, but with none of the exuberance of the Carnivale partygoers. A great shadow loomed to our left and squinting through the mist I could make out a few lights and the distant, sputtering thrums of motors. As we drew nearer, I was shocked to see the name of one of our liners, the Tyche, now a rusted hulk, rammed against the debris of a customs-house at the dock edge. As I looked on in horror, familiar but forgotten voices raised themselves from behind those masks and began a mournful shanty I remembered from my early days at sea:

"And one more day ashore we'll go.
Leave her, Johnny, leave her."

My crew! My first crew! But what a greeting! I ran across the deck to return the refrain, but after a single line their chorus was drowned out by the relentless drone of a foghorn, so loud that its volume knocked me to the deck where I lay prostrated, hands over my ears in agony, until the waters rose so far that I was washed overboard and carried by the tide to be dumped unceremoniously at their feet. Not my most auspicious entrance.

I stood, sodden and shaken, water sloshing around my ankles. No. Not water. Blood, thick and red, swirling around my feet, blood in the puddles and in the canals, lending an eerie red glow to the evening light. I brushed myself down, mask lost in the crimson tide at my feet. Wherever I was, this wasn't Venice, couldn't be Venice, at least not the one I knew from my many visits.

A lone gondola approached, the fog parting reverently around it as the gondolier, cloaked in heavy raiment of shimmering black velvet, drew up to the nearest mooring post. What face lay hidden in the depths of his night-black hood I have only now begun to guess. At that juncture, I was still grimly transfixed by the novelty of the experience and when a single, crooked finger emerged from the long robe and beckoned me approach, I felt helpless to resist.

"Now the rats have gone and we the crew."

We progressed in total silence except for the slow movement of the oar through the waters and that haunting melody whispered through the darkness by the chorus of my first crew. From the cruise ship docks at Santa Chiara through the length of the Canale Grande, under the covered bridge at Rialto. Here the gulls swirled in their hundreds, diving in ones or twos into the deep waters and emerging with cries of victory at the trinkets borne in their beaks, carrying them home to decorate distant nests. It was a disturbing and disgusting site to witness as they fought over meaningless trifles found in the foulest waters, pecking and plucking at the corpse of the city. My cowled gondolier said nothing, and it was clear he would not or could not answer any of the questions burning in my throat. We continued, the solitary travellers on this maritime highway, until he began to slow down at the Salute docks at the stairs of the Basilica di Santa

Maria Della Salute, our Lady of Health. I scrambled to my feet, still full of questions, but eager to escape the macabre and unsettling clutches of the ferryman.

The Basilica was submerged in the low, thick smog which I had first encountered on docking. Here, though, the hue of it was a sickly yellow-tan and it clung to the crumbling church like ancient ivy. Beneath that fog the waters had risen so precariously that they had risen over the top of the steps, just visible in the scarlet-hued waters beneath us. I raised a hand to my mouth in a vain attempt to hold back the sickly sulphurous smog as I clambered out of the gondola, still knee-deep in swirling waters and waist-deep in settled fog and made my way to the altar.

Votive candles commemorating the dead of the plagues which had been visited upon the city lay scattered in this once-holy place, now as forgotten and neglected as the Canal Grande itself. I reached up to find one I could still light, but those that remained were sodden and would not succumb to a flame.

"Where you wish to Christ you'd never been born"

Beneath this great dome, the inhabitants of the city had seemed to make a last stand of sorts. A vigil held in candlelit prayer; a ceremony of innocence now drowned. Now it was teeming with bloated, inundated dead, skeletal hands reaching out of the waters in desperate supplication, hoping for rescue from those on land - who had long forgotten them - and upward to the heavens who seemed to have done likewise. These sepulchral intrusions grabbed at my ankles beneath the surface, trying to drag me down with them to a watery grave. I managed to knock some of them away with a candelabra and scrambled up onto the relative safety of the altar, where my panic subsided and my panting gave way to a wracking, consuming cough. The pollutive mix of the smog, heavy with sulphur and nitrous oxides, fought its way into my mouth in an attempt to do to me what it had done to the building. Limestone statues of the saints had been heavily corroded, so much so that their faces were no longer recognisable. As I spluttered and wheezed and struggled to breathe, the only salvation came in the person of my gondolier. His finger was no longer beckoning but wagging in accusation. I struggled back to the gondola, and we departed in the same silence we had entered as we drifted slowly across to Piazza San Marco.

"Oh, the work was hard, and the voyage was long".

Every column in those fabled colonnades bore the enduring marks of the Acqua Alta: a succession of stains showing the height at which the spring waters had finally ceased their assault. I baulked when I saw that the topmost of these marks was a full arm's length over my head. Pinned to one column in the piazza, flapping audibly in the breeze above the quietly dripping tears of a lost city, was a single flyer, seemingly oblivious to the destruction about it. Roughly translated, it indicated a place where the residents had made a last attempt to hold out against the rising tide, a place on higher ground where the desperate might find shelter. I took it with me, eager to leave this desolation behind and find out what had become of its final inhabitants. I left just as the Acqua Alta sirens began to sound and followed the directions on the flyer, each step taking me to higher ground, lest I become immersed in a tidal flow of blood, salt and water.

The flyer in my hand had almost disintegrated in the damp air by the time I reached the place marked on it. I looked up at the inauspicious building with its faded grandeur, cracked tiles and bust drain pipes. A rivulet of sludge navigated the slick cobbles at my feet. I looked down at the flyer again, making sure I had the address right, squinting at the smudged pulp in the night gloom. Devastated, dejected, disconsolate, I sat on the doorstep, my head in my hands, deciding what to do next. Then I looked up across the muddied gangplanks over the sludge- and trash-strewn alleyway to the low row of buildings opposite.

"In one more day, why we'll go too."

In the fog-choked darkness of the narrow passage, the row of squalid, huddled tenements loomed like a spectral bluff. Not a sound broke the brooding silence save for the screeching of gulls - those verminous vultures of the sea - far overhead in the gloom. Rain beat against the windows and against the roofs, where there were still roofs to beat upon and windows to beat against. It came down in hissing roars, then in whispers, then in loud swishes like sandpaper rubbed on a deck.

Human beings shouldn't have to enter such doors, shouldn't have to stay behind them. No sun or moon ever entered there, no stars, no anything at all. They were worse than the grave, for in the grave is the promise of closure, of or rebirth and another life. Providence orders the grave for all of us; but providence did not order such lodgings as these rat-fat alleys teeming with refuse and the grim, mould-slick halls within which wretched souls are forced to dwell.

I stepped through that threshold. Huddled there against the walls were those last few living inhabitants of this doomed city, rag-clad and cheerless, their red eyes rimmed with sorrow and loss. They looked up, pleading, desperate, until the glimmer of recognition reached the watery grey of their eyes and I realised with horror that they knew who I was.

If the city was doomed, it was I who had doomed it, and in doing so also doomed myself. Those doomed souls, driven to a semblance of life in this abject hovel, knew the architect of their destruction. Sorrow gave way to anger, grief to wrath. One hand raised a fist in fury, then others took up that call and began pelting me with the contents of that beleaguered ruin: broken Murano glassware, rubble groaning with the weight of history and rotted vegetables from the markets of Mestre. I stood in silence and let myself undergo this onslaught with the last scrap of dignity I could muster until, their rage spent, they withdrew to the upper floors in a mindless, pitiless procession of shuffling feet and murmured curses.

I don't know how long I then spent meandering, lost in the depths of the sinking city and my own thoughts. The next thing I recalled is that I was back on that same gondola, passing under the Ponte Dei Sospiri.

The Bridge of Sighs was a sorry sight, evocative now of not even a murmur. There was no beauty here anymore to offer a condemned man his last, fleeting glimpse of La Serenissima. Its Istrian limestone, which had once glistened so white as to elicit such sighs from prisoners on their way to judgement, was pocked with grey splotches of shadowed mould which in combination with the moon-specked blood of the Rio del Palazzo, gave the impression of entering Hell itself. Blackened, tattered banners hung from its barred windows, wherein I spied a single figure, staring back out at me. I recoiled instantly, but then turned back to face that irrevocable fate of an unmasked reflection of myself, in procession to the palace of the Doge. In an instant I was with him in that place, and I stared through the stone bars as my ferryman waited for me on the cool waters as the chorus ushered me forward. Only then did I allow myself a sigh, a single sigh for the lost beauty of the place and another, deeper sigh for the formal trial I knew was about to come.

"And it's time for us to leave her."

Inside the palace a makeshift throne had been crudely fashioned from the rubble and here sat a figure masquerading as Aeacus, he who was famed for his justice in life and now holds court to judge the dead.

Surrounding him were many other figures. My first crew continued their role as tragic chorus while

162

I stared into the faces of my later crews, haggard through overwork and underappreciated, whose gaze I could now barely meet. Along the stone parapets and atop crumbling columns sat the gulls. Voracious yet still aggrieved, fleecing those tourists was my second egregious sin. Neither of these compared to the legion of drowned dead who now stood arrayed to one side of the courtyard, blood lapping at their feet, their number too numerous to count, no longer able to give voice themselves but seemingly content that Aeacus would do it for them.

He did this with a single gesture, a shake of the head which indicated that disappointment so extreme it is rarely seen except upon the face of a parent.

My crew picked up the last refrain of their shanty and the remainder of the crowd carried the chorus until the choice of words finally came crashing down on me like Hokusai's great wave.

"It's time for us to leave her.

Leave her, Johnny, leave her.

For the voyage is done and the winds won't blow."

Not the sea, not the ship, not even the city, but life itself. I'd overstayed my welcome. I begged humbly for one final attempt at contrition which, in their leniency, they granted. It is this last, anguished endeavour that you hold in your hands.

I leave this message in a bottle and consign it to the ocean in the vain hope that benevolent currents carry its confessions and lamentations to the ears of those who need to hear it. One final journey awaits me, one we must all take, one whose ferryman has now been paid in full: in blood and horror, in tumultuous waters and rotting terrors, in life and death. I see it drawing close now through these dark waters, its prow low, its gondolier as silent as the grave itself. The waves withdraw from that ship of endings as it approaches and gather again in its wake, out of respect and sheer terror both. I offer my wretched soul as passage to the infernal ferryman Charon and to the eternal punishments of the underworld that lie beyond the lagoon and across the murky waters of the Styx.

The Twist of a Cork (Stephen Lang)

Theo steadies the globe-shaped bottle on the sand. The thickness of the glass makes the demijohn heavy, and it's a relief to put it down.

Some say it's an odd choice for a storage jar, but the glass helps to lend magnification to the contents. And the bottle being fat and bulbous means it can hold plenty, although the narrow mouth is the one drawback of the design. It's roughly two inches in diameter, twice as wide as a beer bottle, but smaller than the rim of a tankard.

Theo rolls up his shirt sleeves and pulls off his boots. It's always an effort, as they're such a snug fit, and the leather has moulded itself perfectly to the shape of his feet. He places the boots beside the demijohn. Creased and weathered, they stand guard.

The sand has a pasty texture. Theo uses his fingers to burrow down into the clammy wet. It's a lottery what he might uncover today. There's time to try two, maybe three, spots on the beach. He'll mark any failures with heavy stones.

He doesn't dig for long before he sees the gull pecking with its hungry beak. Theo runs towards it, and the bird flies away, already having finished its meal. Or not quite a meal, a human eye providing merely a light snack. Theo feels inside the empty socket of the skull.

The corpse is only half buried, but Theo works up a sweat as he digs out the sand and shells around it. He soon uncovers the right arm. No, the left arm, as the body lies twisted, as if the waves have dumped it here in a rush.

Theo takes the elbow and index finger and gently lifts. The corpse has badly decomposed. The eight carpal bones of the wrist are still intact, along with parts of the forearm - the radius and the ulna. The four fingers of the hand all consist - as expected - of one metacarpal and three phalanges. The thumb is missing.

He has learnt the names of these intricate parts of the human body from his book of anatomy. Next to the demijohn, it's his most treasured possession. He has studied every diagram, cross-checked every name in the index, and made notes in the margins. The book is invaluable to him.

Theo starts to twist off the fingers. They crack as they come loose, requiring about the same strength as it takes to pull apart a lobster. He wipes the bones clean with the hem of his shirt before dropping them into the mouth of the demijohn.

He continues to dig, fully exposing the body and rolling it over. It lies uncomfortably, like a drunkard who has fallen and bashed his brains out.

Theo looks up and down the stretch of the empty beach. Just him and a corpse for company.

His foot tickles. He shouts as he raises his leg, shaking away a string of black seaweed, and almost topples over. A ripple of water turns the seaweed one way and then another. The tide is coming in.

The bones of the right arm are either splintered or missing entirely. It suggests the poor soul died in some calamity before they hit the water. Perhaps this was indeed a drunkard. Perhaps the bravado of drunkenness drew them into a fight, and they became the worse off. One ulna is salvageable. Theo slips it into the mouth of the demijohn.

He feels safer now. Disabled of its upper limbs, the corpse can't drag itself from the sand in his pursuit when he leaves. Stories tell that this is what the dead will try to do. Stories that Theo only half believes. But he will always listen in the way one is inclined to devour a good tale.

The gulls circle above. He fancies he can interpret their cries.

You should not be here.

Do not come here.

Go.

The wind whistles around him as if to answer in agreement, numbing his ears with cold. Theo knows he's spending too long in contemplation as the tide sneaks up, fast closing in from three sides. It could trap him. Leave him to join the corpses. He must hurry.

The grid of bones that make up the right shoulder is still intact, but they'll be too large to fit through the mouth of the demijohn, so Theo begins to gather the components of the left foot. The talus. The tarsals. The feet of the corpse are broad and long. Undoubtedly this was a man.

Theo finishes dismantling the feet. The water now circles him. His boots fall on their sides and take sail as one follows the other into the sea. He reaches for them as they swirl and dance in the waves, but they keep their distance before they sink. He screams an obscenity, knowing the tide has his boots.

Theo's breeches are now wet and heavy from the knees down. He feels for the smooth cork in his pocket. He squeezes it into the mouth of the demijohn with a twist, picks the bottle up and splashes his way inland.

Sharp pebbles nick at his feet as he climbs the zigzag path. He doesn't look back until he reaches the top of the cliff. He likes to mock the beach from this safe position, knowing he has defeated it. He doesn't believe in good luck, despite charms being his business.

Others wouldn't dare to do what he has just done. The locals treat his select pickings as rarities as they refuse to gather the dead and give them a decent burial inland. They believe the bones move in the water at high tide before settling for another night under the sand. So legend has it, but Theo can only detect the natural movement of the roll of the sea below.

The book of anatomy has stayed dry in his back pocket. He opens it and finds the page he wants. He's curious if the finger knuckle has a name, and it has. Theo examines the diagram of the metacarpophalangeal joint before the gull distracts him.

It picks at something, and retreats, before advancing again. The bird is hesitant because its prey is moving. Metacarpal. Phalanges. Four fingers, feeling their way up and over the gorse towards him. Perhaps the stories are true after all. Theo kicks the hand, forgetting he's barefoot. But it's a good kick when his toes connect, and it drops out of sight.

Theo thinks of what his mother used to say to him. It helped to make him such a sceptic. *Just your imagination, Theo.* But he knows what he has just seen.

The bones inside the demijohn stand in line like mismatched toothpicks. Theo has made a fair haul today to sell as charms. Tomorrow, he intends to profit from the bones of the drowned. He may soon afford to eat lobster again.

***

The buildings loom above on four sides - a church, a bell house, a municipal bank, and other unidentifiable stone structures. The crowds hurry towards the centre of the square as one entity.

Theo pushes his way through. He must find a pitch, his own space, somewhere to put the demijohn on display, but he's only met with glances of contempt from the city goers. He knows what they're thinking.

You should not be here.

Do not come here.

Go.

The traders wear colourful scarves, bowler hats and quarter-length coats. They shout in sing-song voices, and the competition to attract the crowd's attention is fierce.

Theo fastens the top button of his shirt. He hand combs his hair. His breeches are still damp, and his feet are black with dirt. He should have worked on his presentation, but this is the best he can do until he can sell a charm.

He forces his way into the crowd, knowing he can shout as loud as the others if he tries. *Good luck. Wishes. Charms*. He repeats his new mantra but turns no heads.

Theo soon loses his footing, submerged in a sea of bodies. He cradles the demijohn as he falls, saving it from smashing. Damn his pride. The demijohn is all that matters. He can hardly breathe.

He's hesitant to move should he be kicked back down to the ground, so he squats, his arms wrapped around the demijohn until a strong hand reaches for his arm and pulls him out of the throng.

Thin reddish hair straddles the top of the man's head, and the rest hangs long around his shoulders. A white stubble covers his pockmarked cheeks. His face has seen many years, many seasons. His silver-buttoned black trench coat suggests a degree of wealth, a higher station to the traders.

"What's your name, lad?"

His voice is gruff, hoarse. Croaky from too much tobacco.

"Theo. Thank you, sir. And yours?"

The man points at the demijohn.

"May I?"

He grits his brown teeth as he traces a finger across the glass.

"I'm Gaspard," he says.

Gaspard examines the bones. He squints as he tilts his head. At last, Theo may have a customer.

"Good luck charms," he says. "I'm here to sell them."

Gaspard feels the top of the cork and hesitates. Perhaps he senses a warning in Theo's eyes.

"Superstition," he says. "Yes?" He spits on the ground. "Cut-off fishing villages. Is that where you're from?" Theo bows his head in assent. "Ha! I knew it. Remoteness breeds ignorance."

Theo begins to relate yesterday's events as if in defence. He feels he has to top and tail them as a story. He also embellishes what happened. The fingers on the gorse. Other hands, torsos, half bodies climbing to the top of the cliff in his pursuit. He still has an imagination.

"Such is the risk taken in disturbing the dead," he says.

Perhaps this stranger will buy all Theo's charms on the back of a good tale. But Gaspard grunts dismissively and turns away. Theo picks up the demijohn and follows him to a row of teak cabinets. Gaspard sorts through a ring of keys, finds a brass skeleton, and unlocks the first.

"This is what people want," he says. "Curiosities. Science. Not fanciful stories."

"I'm interested in science," says Theo.

Gaspard gives another dismissive grunt, so Theo shows him the book of anatomy. He indicates where he has made notes to prove himself a keen student.

"Science, then," says Gaspard. "If you are so interested."

He opens the cabinet and takes out a glass bottle. It's smaller than Theo's demijohn but has a wider mouth covered by a brass cap. The foetus inside floats in a clear solution. It has two misshapen heads. Its hands are raised in surrender, apologetic at its failure to live beyond - what - weeks? They're unformed hands - four webbed fingers and a thumb - that look more like mittens.

171

Mittens on a child that never lived, although Theo is sure the arms sway in the solution to some tune inaudible to him.

There is nothing like this in the book of anatomy. It catalogues the dead and gone but says little about what could be.

"I'll take that demijohn off your hands," says Gaspard. "I could make use of it. It's not worth anything, but I'll give you something as a fair exchange."

Gaspard gestures to a cabin trunk. The wood is worn and scratched, suggesting many voyages, but Theo senses he's about to be short-changed as he rummages through the contents. A threadbare blanket. Rusted hand tools. A coil of rope. A collection of candlesticks. And a pair of boots.

"Take them if you want," says Gaspard.

Gaspard twists out the cork of the demijohn. He shakes the contents into the gutter, and the bones rattle out. A dog runs over to inspect them.

Theo sits by the kerbside and feels the smoothness of the leather. Tight and snug, the boots are a perfect fit.

Meet the Authors

Rie Sheridan Rose

Rie multitasks. A lot. Her short stories appear in numerous anthologies, including Killing It Softly Vol. 1 & 2, Hides the Dark Tower, Dark Divinations and On Fire. She has authored twelve novels, six poetry chapbooks and lyrics for dozens of songs. She is also editor-in-chief for Mocha Memoirs Press and editor for the Thirteen O' Clock imprint of Horrified Press. She tweets as @RieSheridanRose.

Olivia Arieti

Olivia lives in Torre del Lago Puccini, Italy, with her family. She writes drama, poetry and fiction. Her stories have appeared in several magazines and anthologies including, *Enchanted Conversations, Enchanted Tales Literary Magazine, Fantasia Divinity Magazine, Forgotten Tomb Press, Horrified Press, Infective Ink, Pandemonium Press, Sirens Call Publications, Blood Song Books, Black Hare Press, Pussy Magic Magazine, Stormy Island Publishing, Breaking Rules Publishing, Scarlet Leaf Review, Iron Faerie Publishing, Dark Dossier Magazine, Paramour Ink Press, Raven and Drake Publishing*.

Jackk N. Killington

Jackk N. Killington lives in Missouri where he writes stories and Novels when he isn't working and helping his roommate. Jackk has been published in multiple mediums branching from Webzines to Anthologies and magazines.

Jason R. Frei lives in Eastern Pennsylvania where he works as a therapist with children and adolescents. He writes speculative fiction culled from the experiences of his life and those he works with and blends science fiction, fantasy and horror into new creations. His flash story "The Garden" will be featured in the horror anthology *99 Tiny Terrors* by Pulse Publishing and his short story "Some of the Parts" will be featured in the horror anthology *Toilet Zone 3: The Royal Flush* by Hellbound Books Publishing. Visit him online: https://facebook.com/odinstones.

Ian McKinley

Ian McKinley is a Scot, living in Switzerland and spending much of his time in Japan. A professional scientist and fan of all forms of science fiction in books, comics and movies, he decided at the turn of the century to extend from writing text books and technical papers to the new challenges of fiction. Writing occurs mainly during long vacations spent diving, skiing and exploring exotic locations, which provide inspiration and settings for his books.

He writes novels set in the middle of this century, major social and environmental changes along with rapidly developing technology forming the backdrop for action thrillers written for a mature audience. The characters play a central role, tacitly

174

establishing the cultural changes resulting from increasing sexual permissiveness and growth in the power of mega-corporations at the expense of national governments. As Ian has a wide overview of the most recent developments in science and technology, the future worlds described are credible and, given their generally dystopic nature, maybe worryingly so.

Carl Hughes

Carl is a writer and journalist who has worked for the national and provincial press in the UK and has had his articles published worldwide, from the UK to Australia, India to the US. His fiction has appeared in many anthologies and magazines and he has won numerous writing competitions. He specialises in writing about the offbeat and bizarre, with a special love of horror and *Twilight Zone*-type stories. He is married and lives in Norfolk with wife Linda.

Sashi Kadapa

Based in Pune, India, Shashi Kadapa is the managing editor of ActiveMuse, a journal of literature. Thrice nominated for Pushcart Prize, he is a two-time award winner of the IHRAF, NY short story competition. His works: http://www.activemuse.org/Shashi/Shashi_Pubs.html

SJ Townend

SJ hopes that her stories take the reader on a journey to often a dark place and only sometimes back again.

SJ won the Secret Attic short story contest (Spring 2020), has had fiction published with Sledgehammer Lit Mag, Hash Journal, Ghost Orchid Press, Bandit Fiction, Black Hare Press, Black Petals Horror Magazine, Ellipsis Zine, Gravely Unusual, Gravestone Press, Holy Flea, Horla Horror, and was long listed for the Women on Writing non-fiction contest in 2020.

She has also written and self-published two dark mystery novels, both of which are available to purchase on Amazon: (Tabitha Fox Never Knocks, Twenty-Seven and the Unkindness of Crows).

Follow her on Twitter: @SJTownend

Thomas M. Malafarina

(www.ThomasMMalafarina.com) has published seven horror novels, as well as seven collections of horror short stories. He has also published a book of often strange single panel cartoons called Yes I Smelled It Too, as well as a Microsoft based technical manual called Link-Tuit. He has written and published more than 200 short stories. All of his horror books have been published through Hellbender Books an imprint of Sunbury Press. (www.Sunburypress.com).

Stuart Holland

Stuart is the owner of Fiction4All, a golf enthusiast (especially the 19th hole) and has written in the genres of crime/mystery, thrillers and suspense, and has now turned his hand to horror. His books are available from fiction4all.com in both digital and print editions. His other interests include conspiracy theories, the Knights Templars and he has a fascination for the paranormal and supernatural. Which may explain why he wrote 2020-Wipeout a couple of years before Covid-19 had ever been heard about!

Liam A. Spinage

Liam is a former philosophy student, former archaeology educator and former police clerk who spends most of his spare time on the beach gazing up at the sky and across the sea while his imagination runs riot.

Stephen Lang

Stephen Lang has harboured a lifetime love of all things terrifying. His short stories have appeared in the BHF Book of Horror Stories (BHF Books), Step Into the Light (Bag of Bones Press), Dark Stories Volumes 3 and 4 (Gravestone Press), Fear Forge (Horrorsmith Publishing), Halloweenthology: Día de Muertos (Wicked Shadow Press) and online at The Sirens Call and Unveiling Nightmares. Stephen lives in Bristol and is a member of the Horror Writers Association.